You NEEDED Me

A Love Story

2

A NOVEL BY

SHVONNE LATRICE

Published by Leo Sullivan Presents

www.leolsullivan.com

This is an original work of fiction. Names, characters, places and incidents are either products of the author's imagination or are used fictitiously and any resemblance to actual persons, living or dead is entirely coincidental.

Contains explicit language & adult themes suitable for ages 16+

CHAPTER ONE

Kimberlyn

"All them niggas can stay in the trash, right along with Britain's ass," Goldie rolled her eyes.

Britain was harassing Goldie on the low, or at least he thought it was on the low, but she showed us all his begging ass texts. This dude had a bitch but was chasing Goldie. I shook my head as I thought about it.

We finally chose a movie, The Wood, and began to watch it. Halfway through the film, the UPS man beat on the screen door, before dropping a package. I hated that he did that shit because it always scared the fuck out of me.

Since I'd recently placed an order online, I hopped up and went outside to get it. Closing the door behind me, I walked out onto the porch to grab the box. I then went down the steps to go into the mailbox to make sure we'd gotten all the mail from earlier.

WHAM!

While I was looking in the mailbox, I was suddenly struck across the back of the head with a heavy ass object. Tears immediately came out of my eyes as I became dizzy. Right when I was about to turn around, I collapsed to the floor in pain, listening to the attacker pant heavily. I tried to adjust my sight so I could see who it was as I turned over.

WHAM!

Another strike from the blurry figure dressed in all black. They kicked my leg, and before I could say anything, I blacked out.

CHAPTER ONE

Matikah Jacobson

"Damn, what the fuck is taking Kimberlyn so long?" Goldie frowned.

We'd paused the movie because she left out to get a package, but about five minutes had already passed and she still hadn't come back. I wasn't worried. I just wanted her to hurry the fuck up so we could finish watching the movie.

"Let me go check," I said, getting up from the couch.

I walked to the door, and opened it to see Kimberlyn lying on the ground by the mailbox. *What the fuck,* I thought.

"Kimberlyn!" I shouted as I rushed down the porch steps and over to her. "Oh my gosh!" I hollered when I saw blood covering her hairline, and that she was clearly passed out. "Ma! Ma! Someone call 911!" I shouted when I saw Goldie and Summer come to the door. I felt like I was about to have a heart attack because she looked dead.

"What the fuck happened?" Goldie screeched as she jogged over.

"Just call 911!" I responded.

"I'm calling now," Summer sighed as she dialed on her iPhone. My grandmother came to the door, and like Goldie, she raced down to see why Kimberlyn was lying on the ground with blood on her fucking head.

"My baby! What the hell?!" my grandmother yelled as she dropped down next to Goldie and I to inspect Kimberlyn's wounds.

"They're on their way," Summer approached us.

About ten minutes later, an ambulance came speeding down our street with their siren blasting. Neighbors began to exit their houses to see why they were here, as the EMTs rolled a stretcher out the back of the truck. I'd never seen so many people outside at once, but that was nosey ass Roxbury for you.

"What happened?" one of them asked as they lifted Kimberlyn onto the gurney, and began checking her pulse. "We have a pulse."

"I-I don't know, we just came outside and she was lying there like that!" I explained to him, and he nodded before wheeling her away. "Let's go!" I said before running inside to get the keys to my car. I hated Lendsey, but I was definitely thankful for this damn car he'd purchased me.

The four of us piled into my vehicle, and then drove to Massachusetts General Hospital where Kimberlyn was headed. We got there only a short while after the ambulance, and thankfully, they'd already taken her to the back to tend to her. *Lord, please let my cousin be okay,* I silently prayed.

I was going crazy wondering who the fuck could've done such a thing to my cousin. She didn't have beef with anyone at all. Everyone loved Kimberlyn, so who the hell would want to kill her or harm her in that way? All that blood was sickening to see, and to know someone left her for dead like that had me furious. I wanted to find someone to blame so I could whoop their ass.

"Lord, I can't deal with this shit right now." My grandmother rocked back and forth as we waited in the lobby area.

"Calm down, Ma, they said she had a pulse."

"Matikah, whomever did this was trying to kill her, think about that. She lived this time, but who is to say that the person won't come back, huh?"

I made eye contact with Goldie when my grandmother said that, and I could tell she was just as scared and worried as I. Yeah Kimberlyn lived, but we needed to find out who did this, and most importantly why. I didn't want to wait until they finally succeeded and murdered her.

A little over half an hour had passed when I heard footsteps coming down the hall at a very quick pace. Their voices sounded distressed, and I wondered who it was. The voice of the person they were with sounded familiar, but I wasn't sure just yet. Hopefully, whoever it was had some information that would be helpful.

"Where is she?" TQ appeared with Lendsey standing behind him. Lendsey and I made eye contact, but I promptly looked away from him.

"They have her in the back, and they will let us know something soon, TQ," Summer responded to him.

Obviously that wasn't good enough, because he stormed to the nurse's desk and slammed his hand down on the countertop so that she would turn around. She looked at him like he was crazy, and then scooted her chair closer to him. I could tell she was ignorant and wanting to put him in his place as soon as she could.

"Can I help you, sir?" she raised her brow, ready to get an attitude with him. I prayed that she didn't because she had no idea who she was dealing with right now.

"I need to know what the fuck is up with Kimberlyn Harrey."

After looking up some information, the nurse said, "Sir, she just got here about forty minutes ago. I don't know—"

"Well you better get real fuckin' knowledgeable before we have a problem up in this bitch! You don't want it with me, ma! Now get yo' lazy ass up and go find out an update or some shit! Call somebody or something!" TQ barked, prompting Lendsey to stop staring at me and go over there to calm his brother down.

"Sir, I don't know—"

"Aye man, come on!" Lendsey hollered when TQ pulled his gun out and pressed it to the nurse's forehead, causing her head to tilt back a bit.

"That's my shorty in there, and you need to find out if she's okay or not. That girl is my world, and without her I ain't got nothing to lose. I will kill yo' ass right here and sleep tight tonight," TQ stated calmly, with the pistol still prodding the young nurse's forehead.

Everyone was quiet as hell, hoping the nurse complied, because he would surely blow her brains out in this public hospital. I was just thanking God that there weren't any people around to see this catastrophe. Another nurse came walking up, but when she saw crazy ass TQ with a gun aimed at her co-worker, her shady ass made a quick U-turn.

My grandmother looked at me with bulged eyes, and I knew she was thinking that TQ was out of his mind. He *was* out of his mind right now, and we really couldn't blame him.

"Le-let me place a call," the nurse stammered.

"Thank you, and don't try to pull a fast one, shorty."

The nurse dialed on her phone, talked for a few minutes, and then finally hung up.

"She had a bad concussion, but she's gonna live. They're working on her, and she is still knocked out, but she will be fine, sir. No visits will be allowed tonight," the nurse explained. She was still afraid because her voice was trembling. It was probably because TQ was still holding his gun as if it were a harmless cellphone or something.

"No visits?" my grandmother stood up and walked over.

"No ma'am, I'm sorry. Ms. Harrey is still out of it anyway, and they don't want anyone coming in to see her. Plus, they believe they will be working on her all night. She should be allowed to accept visits in the morning. But please, sit down and wait for the doctor to come out and tell you this, because I could lose my job for what I've just divulged."

My grandmother, Lendsey, and TQ all came to sit down and wait. Finally, after twenty minutes, the doctor came out and told us the exact same thing as the nurse. He told us that the brick was heavy enough to knock her out, but whoever assaulted her wasn't very strong, or didn't use much force. The reason she was bleeding was because the brick scraped her skin, not because of any serious head injury. We all pretended it was our first time hearing it, and then exited the hospital.

"Aye, Matikah!" Lendsey called out to me as I walked to my car with Summer, Goldie, and my grandmother.

"What?" I turned to him as they kept walking.

"I umm, I just want to make sure you're okay."

"I'm fine."

"Good, good. I'm sorry about your cousin, shorty, I know this is killing you." He stepped closer and tried to rub my face, but I turned away. "Matikah, I miss—"

"Lendsey, save it, please. Accept that it's done, okay?" With that, I walked to my car and pulled out of the hospital.

That nigga really thought I would let him comfort me? Please!

Monica Jordan

An hour and a half earlier...

I hurriedly pulled into Gang's driveway, before shutting off the engine and darting to the door. I wanted to hurry up and change clothes before he got home, because he would for sure be suspicious of my all black outfit. I was a colorful girl, and usually only stepped out in sandals and heels. That was a far cry from the all black Dr. Martens, tights, and turtleneck I was wearing.

I know what you're wondering; if I'm the one that knocked Gang's little innocent princess across the head. I sure and the fuck did, and I pray I killed the bitch. The brick I had was heavier than I expected, so I couldn't deliver the blows as hard as I wanted to. But on the bright side, I did see blood so I should have done some damage. And if she didn't die this time, I would catch that ass again. I would come for her until I put her in the ground.

I hated Kimberlyn with every fiber of my being. Gang was mine before he even knew her, and I knew she understood that he was mine, yet she still allowed him to court her. What kind of shit is that? Home wrecking ass bitch. She tried to pretend like she believed that Gang and I were just friends, but she knew the real deal. Kimberlyn was no dummy, and if she did actually believe that Gang wasn't fucking me, then I feel even worse for the hoe.

I also hated that she thought she was big and bad sometimes. Whenever I would try to throw small jabs at her, she would throw them right back and act like she was really gonna beat my ass or something. Girl, bye! She won't be beating anybody's ass these days, now that she got knocked the fuck out, or hopefully killed.

I smiled to myself as I walked up the huge staircase in Gang's house. Now that Kimberlyn had left him high and dry for that impeccable ass TQ, I was able to damn near live here. Before, he would only let me come over if Kimberlyn wouldn't, or if he wanted to fuck. I hated that he only called when he needed me, but I loved him so I will always be there when he calls.

Speaking of TQ though, I couldn't really blame Kimberlyn for getting with him. I mean having an encounter with a Quinton was a once in a lifetime chance. And if they wanted to fuck you too, you'd be a fool to pass up the opportunity. Not only was moving on a smart choice because of who TQ was, but it also could have prevented her from being killed this evening. Too bad she just couldn't be happy with what she had.

I got to the bathroom and turned on the water so I could take a nice hot victory shower. I undressed down to nothing, and shook my head at how beautiful I was; smooth light skin, short curly hair, and a banging ass body. A lot of people said I looked like a thicker Tanaya Henry, but I looked way better in my opinion. To make a long story short, I was a bad bitch, and really had no business chasing behind

Gang or any other man for that matter.

I will admit that when I met Gang I was only into him because of who he was. I mean everyone knew who Gang was in Boston. Like he always said, he was the fucking king out here. Being on his arm was something I could have only dreamed of at the time, and funny enough, it came true. I met him at a club one night, and from there we'd become close. All I did was strut by his VIP in my skintight white dress, and he was drooling like Scooby Doo did for his Scooby snacks. We slept together that night, and damn was the shit good. He had a nice big dick and knew how to work it. Naturally over time we got to know one another, and I fell in love with Saadiq. I no longer cared about him being the biggest kingpin in Massachusetts, I only wanted to be with him for him.

He was on that same page, too, until Kimberlyn showed up and completely stole his attention. I had no problem with Gang sleeping with groupies here and there because what could I expect? He was a sexy man with a lot of money and women throwing themselves at him 24/7. For me to expect him to remain faithful would be me living in fool's paradise. My mama always told me, a man with money will never be faithful. Shit a man with a good ten dollars had hoes, so imagine a man with much more. All men cheated anyway, it was just how they went about it. As long as the bitch didn't approach me, I was good. I didn't like messy philanderers.

After my long wonderful shower, I picked up my cellphone and dialed my best friend, Lira. I wanted to tell her about my wonderful day and what I'd done. I was smiling so hard my cheeks were beginning to get sore.

"Hello?" she answered, and I could tell she'd just woken up from a nap.

"Bitch, sit up, I have some shit to tell you!" I giggled and slipped my panties up. I laid back on the bed, topless, waiting for her to get situated.

"Alright, what's up?"

"I got that bitch."

"Who, Kimberlyn? How?"

"Yes, that hoe. I knocked her upside the head with a brick. She fell out, and blood was everywhere. Hopefully the bitch is dead so I can get back to doing me." I know blood wasn't everywhere, but I was a bit of an embellisher.

"What the fuck, Monica? Tell me you're joking!"

Her reaction caught me off guard like a muthafucka, because I'd been telling her for the longest that I was gonna get at Kimberlyn.

"No, I'm not joking! I told you she was gonna hear from me and it was gonna be violent, so why are you so astonished right now?" I sat up.

"I thought you were just blowing smoke! What if you killed that girl, Monica? You can go to jail for life or get the death sentence!"

"Calm down! You are so damn dramatic! No one saw me, and no one will ever know because Gang will protect me. The only way someone will find out is if you tell, and you won't, right?" I raised a brow as if she could see me.

"You know I won't, Monica," she sighed. "You know, you're doing all this, for what? All Gang is gonna do is find a new woman to chase after. You know that, right?"

"What the fuck are you talking about, stupid? He won't go looking again because he knows I'm where he wants to be! He already told me he only wanted to fuck Kimberlyn, okay?"

"Then why did you feel the need to try and murder the girl if he only wanted sex?"

"Because he was taking too long to get it, and he was spending too much time talking and thinking about her! I was tired of it!"

"No, because you know deep down that he's lying to you, Monica! He is lying! He wants to be with her, not you, and you need to accept that! You are too smart and beautiful for this, Mo! Stop wasting time with a man who will never be with you like that, and go find a man who wants you and only you!"

"No man wants one woman, Lira."

"Stop with that 'all men cheat' bullshit, Monica. Look, you need to move on and let Gang turn some other bitch crazy, not you. You have a good job, a degree, and you're beautiful; you can be with someone else."

"I'm already twenty-eight, Lira, I need to get married."

"Exactly my point, Monica. You're wasting your years with him when he's never gonna marry you, ever. He's only holding onto you until he finds someone else. Believe me, if Kimberlyn or any other woman agrees to be with him, he will leave you. And if TQ finds out what you did, you're gonna lose your life. And for what? For a boy who isn't man enough to sit you down and be real about his feelings?"

"You know what, Lira? No wonder you don't have a man. And you will never have one until you lose weight, so good luck with that!" I hated to insult my friend, but she was pissing me off.

"Bye, Monica." She hung up.

I slammed my phone into the bed right when Gang walked into the bedroom.

"Hey, baby!" I squealed and rushed over to him. I tried to hug him but he nudged me off lightly. "I can't hug you?"

"I'm not in the hugging mood, aight?" he sighed and plopped down on the bed.

"What happened, honey?"

"I got word that shorty is in the hospital."

"Shorty?"

"Kimberlyn. Fuck!" he shouted. His eyes said so many things that had never come out of his mouth. He looked like a husband who'd lost his wife. He loved her. He was expressing his love for her through his emotions right in front of me.

"Saa, it's gonna be okay. I'm sure she will be fine. And if not, hey, that's what she gets for leaving you, right?" I chuckled lightly as I knelt down in front of him. Before my other knee hit the carpet, he had his large hand wrapped around my neck.

"Watch yo' fucking mouth, aight? The only person needing to die is that nigga, TQ. Don't you ever speak ill of her again or I will bust ya head wide open, Monica," he gritted so angrily that I was sure his eyes turned blood red. I just nodded so he let me go. "Bend over," he had the nerve to say to me. "Take ya fucking panties off and bend over!" he hollered since I hadn't moved.

I slowly stood to my feet and removed my panties. Once I did, he yanked my arm and threw me face down onto the bed. I listened to him unbuckle his pants, before roughly placing me to my knees and sliding inside.

"Fuck. This is the only reason I let you get by with that smart ass mouth," he grunted as he pumped in and out of me.

Lira was right; I would never be enough for him. I was simply a placeholder until something else better came along.

Tarenz "TQ" Quinton

A week and a half later...

"How are you feeling, shorty?"

I walked into my bedroom to see Kimberlyn sitting in my bed. She was wearing her short nightshirt, holding a cup of tea. Her long, dark hair was disheveled, but she was beautiful nonetheless.

"I'm okay. I would like for you to take me home, please." She set the tea on the nightstand.

"Why?" I frowned.

"I just want to be alone for a little while, is all."

I sat down on the edge of the bed to look into her face. Everything had gone back to normal fairly quickly, but she had a small scar along her hairline. It wasn't really noticeable unless you looked closely at it.

"I don't want you to be alone. I don't want you at your grandmother's right now, Kimberlyn. You're staying here with me. My driver will take you to class in the morning."

She didn't have an option at the moment. She was staying here with me and that was it. I wasn't sure who had hit her over the head, but I was about to find out. And whoever it was would wish they were dead by the time I got to them.

"I know it was probably one of your bitches!" she said in a low tone and nudged my face, as tears began to well up in her eyes. I held her hand against my face to kiss her palm really quickly. I was so in love with this girl that it was scaring me a little bit.

"Kimberlyn, I don't have any bitches. And any girls that I did mess with for one, don't know where you live, and two, they know better."

"Hayden probably knows where I live."

"She probably does, but Hayden is no fool, ma. She would never do something like this because she knows I wouldn't hesitate to take care of her. And baby, Hayden understands that she and I weren't even like that."

"She didn't seem to understand that, that day in the mall."

I scooted closer to her and tried to kiss her lips, but she pushed me back lightly. Grabbing her small wrists into my hands, I pinned them down and leaned in again. Every time I got close, she would turn her face away. Finally, I gripped her chin and forced a kiss on her soft lips. I'd only kissed her once since she'd been out, and I missed it funny enough.

We kept kissing until she was lying on her back. I quickly pulled her nightshirt over her head to expose her naked body, and then removed the boxers I was wearing. Climbing between her legs, I bent down a little to kiss her flat stomach. I was so worried that something had happened to the baby she was carrying, but I was ecstatic to find out everything was all good.

I wiggled my way inside her body, and watched her throw her head back in pain and pleasure. She was so beautiful, and the more time I spent around her, the stronger my feelings for her became. Moving in and out of her, I just stared down into her face with my upper body in the push up position almost.

"I love you, baby," I whispered and leaned down to kiss on her neck, cheek, and lips. "I won't let anything else happen to you."

Pinning her hands behind her head, I sped up my thrusts as she called out to the high heavens. I loved the sound of her moans; they were so sexy to me for some reason. Usually a woman's moans would go unnoticed, but Kimberlyn's intensified the sex for me.

"Mmm, uuhhh, uhhh!" she whimpered loudly as I plowed into her feverishly. Soon after, I was exploding inside of her. "I love you T—" Before she could finish, my tongue was down her throat.

Someone was gonna pay for that shit… I just hoped it wasn't Hayden.

***

Inside the huge parking structure, I waited for Hayden to come to her car. She got off work about five minutes ago, and I was sure she'd be entering the structure pretty soon. I'd broken into her car, so I was sitting in the back seat already, just waiting to question her and possibly bust her over the head if need be.

I didn't think Hayden had anything to do with what happened to Kimberlyn, but she did approach her that day at Copley Mall. Hayden knew better, but the fact that she came at my girl with some bullshit had me wondering if she'd lost her cotton picking mind or not. If she did, she was also about to lose her life. I didn't play games like that, and if anybody knew that, Hayden did.

I watched her walk to the car, open the door, and then throw her big purse into the passenger seat. Sliding in, she cranked the car up, and reached to turn on the air conditioner. As she peeled her jacket off, I eased my pistol between the seat and the headrest, jamming it into the nape of her neck.

"Ah!" she yelped when she felt the cold metal poking her.

"Turn the car off," I hissed, clenching my teeth.

"Tarenz?" She looked into her rearview mirror with a frown.

"Cut the shit off right now, Hayden." Once she did as I asked, I cocked the gun and began to question her. "Did you fuck with my girl?"

"TQ, you know I wou—"

"It's a simple yes or no question, Hayden. Did you fuck with her or not? Don't lie, because if you lie that will only hurt you in the end. I will find out the truth."

"No, Tarenz! I did not touch her! You know I wouldn't do anything like that!" she began to cry. Dropping her face into her hands, I watched her body jerk violently as she wept like her life was over.

Pulling my gun back and securing it in my jacket, I exited the car and got in on the passenger side. I didn't quite know what to say to her. Hayden and I were always cool and nothing more, and I'd never seen her cry or anything like that. In addition to that, I wasn't the nigga you wanted consoling you. I was the type to put a gun to your head and tell you to chill out and stop crying. That's how I was raised and that shaped who I was. I didn't like all that sappy shit.

"Hayden, come on, man, chill out. Did I scare you?" I quizzed, even though I knew I had. Hayden was no weak bitch though, so that couldn't have been why she was crying this hard.

"No you hur-hurt me!" she stammered and wiped her drenched cheeks with the back of her small hand.

"Hurt you how?"

"How do you think, Tarenz? This whole Kimberlyn situation! What about us, huh? What about you never being able to be a boyfriend!" she shouted. For the first time in forever, I realized Hayden had deeper feelings for me than she let on. She always made it seem like she was joking around with me and that she really didn't care, but I was seeing that, that was all a facade.

"Shorty, you have a man," was all I could think to say. Call me dumb and blind, but I was perplexed right now. I thought she just loved the dick down, not my ass.

"Because you didn't want to be with me! I told you all you had to do was say the word and I would leave him. That offer still stands, Tarenz." She rubbed my bicep, but I moved it away from her. It was a reflex and not something I did on purpose.

"Hayden, I'm sorry, ma, but I don't want a relationship—"

"But you're with Kim—"

"With you. I don't want a relationship with you. And when I told you I wasn't the boyfriend type, I was being honest… at that time.

Honestly, I'm still not the type to be someone's man but I'm willing to try."

"For her," she scoffed and shook her head as she stared straight ahead.

"Yes, for her."

"You really ain't shit, Tarenz Quinton."

"I'm not shit but I told yo' hard headed ass countless times that I would never be with you. How the fuck can you blame me because you decided to still stick around, huh? Then you're the one who pretended like you were good with our sex-only situation when you really weren't. And you're the one who has a nigga but is still letting me fuck! So if we really wanna talk about people who ain't shit, you're right in line behind me, ma."

"Okay! Okay fine, you can be with her, but just give me some of your time."

"Nah." I shook my head and reached for the lever to open the door.

"Please, TQ!" she grabbed my arm.

"Fuck off me, I told yo' ass no," I stated calmly but snatched my arm away.

Exiting the car, I rounded the back of the vehicle and started off. I heard the click clack of some heels, so I looked over my shoulder, to see Hayden power walking after me. She fell to the ground, and wrapped her arms around my ankle, making me stop in my tracks. Was she serious right now?

"Please, Tarenz! Don't do this!" she sobbed, while bear hugging my leg.

"Hayden, get the fuck up!" I barked as I subtly watched people stare at us. Why wouldn't they stare? Hayden looked like a damn fool!

"No! Not until you agree to give me some of your time! I need you, Tarenz! I love you and you cannot do this to me!" she screeched so loudly that it echoed all over the floor of the structure.

"Get up, get the fuck up." I bent down, gripped her skinny shoulders, and yanked her ass up with force. Squeezing her biceps, I stared into her eyes intensely before saying, "Leave me the fuck alone, Hayden. And if I hear about or see you bothering my girl, I will kill you."

"How can you say you will kill me so calmly like it's nothing?" she sniffled.

"Because it ain't. One bullet between your eyes and I will be good."

I let her go and then proceeded to my car. Initially, I was happy to know that Hayden hadn't been involved with Kimberlyn's assault, because I didn't want to have to kill the bitch. But maybe I would have to anyway.

Preston "Peel" Thomas

A couple hours later...

"Who do you think could have done some shit like that?" I looked to Gang as I passed him the blunt.

"Nigga, I have no idea. But shit, I bet you it was one of them hoes that TQ has been smashing behind Kimberlyn's back."

"Maybe if you let her know that, she will be more fond of you," I smiled at him, and he nodded with a grin.

"True. But damn, if I could just find out who it was exactly, that would help my case. If I could bring her the name of the jump off, she would be more likely to believe me."

"Call Jayce, that's TQ's best friend and he knows all the bitches he's been with, I'm sure."

"I will do that," he nodded.

"Aight, I'm about to go to Hayden's crib. Let me know if that nigga Jayce mentions her as one of TQ's bed buddies," I half joked.

"Yeah, aight," Gang chuckled.

A part of me still felt like Hayden was fucking him, and I kind of wanted to have that nigga ask Jayce specifically. Only thing was, I wasn't sure if I wanted to know the answer. The whole situation had already caused me to do something I regretted, so I needed to get it under control. I wasn't even sure of how I would react if I found out, but I was sure it wouldn't be pretty.

I made it to Hayden's condo about twenty minutes later, after stopping to get some food for us. She was always hungry, and I learned my lesson the last time I came over without any food for her. You would think she was pregnant with the way that she acted. I wish she were pregnant.

Walking into her house, I saw one of her mood candles burning, so I knew she was home already. I placed the food on the counter, and then went into the fridge to see what she had to drink. I could hear her talking on the phone in the bathroom, and the worst in me wanted to listen. I hated to be so distrustful, but I was about to propose to this girl and I needed to know. I couldn't marry her thinking she was fucking another man, especially TQ. Her messing with him would be the ultimate embarrassment.

I removed my tennis shoes, and crept up to listen at the bathroom door. I could hear in her voice that she was crying, which really piqued my interest.

"He had me looking like a fool, Ingrid. I was literally begging him while holding onto his leg like some peasant!" she sobbed. *What the fuck?* I thought.

She had Ingrid on speakerphone, and this was the one time I was happy that we didn't live together. She thought she was alone, so she felt comfortable enough to have this conversation on speakerphone.

My heart almost stopped as I continued to listen to her conversation.

"I told you to give him some time, Hayden. He would've gotten tired of Kimberlyn eventually, and would have been knocking on your door. You just hurt your chances of ever being with him."

BOOF!

I couldn't take it anymore, so I burst into the bathroom wearing a menacing look. I was livid, and more furious than I ever knew I could be. She'd been playing me this whole time and I'd known it. All the niggas in the world yet she chose that one.

"Ho-how long have you been at the door?" she stuttered with tears and makeup running down her face.

"Long enough. Hang up the fucking phone."

"Preston—"

"Hang up the fucking phone!" I roared so loudly that it felt like thunder in my chest.

"Hayden, do not hang up!" Ingrid yelled through the phone.

I snatched it from her hand, threw it to the floor, and began crushing it with my bare foot. I was so mad, that my foot was strong enough to crush the iPhone to little pieces.

She stood up, and I grabbed her by the neck before slamming her into the wall roughly. She cried out in pain as I continued to slam her small body into the wall like a rag doll. There were so many things I wanted to do to this bitch that I didn't know where to start.

"You got me out here looking stupid!" I backhanded her and she flew into the tub.

"No! Preston, please, let me ex—"

WHAM! WHAM! WHAM!

I punched and slapped her continuously, not caring that blood was flying everywhere and getting all over me. All I was imagining was her getting fucked by that nigga the same way I fucked her. The people in the hood were supposed to respect me and fear me, yet they were probably laughing at me because I had a hoe for a girlfriend. Not to mention that nigga TQ. He was probably enjoying the fact that he had my girl. All these thoughts caused me to go in on her face as if I were Sugar Ray Robinson.

I'd finally had enough of whooping her ass, so I stood up to stare down at her. Her face was beat the fuck up. I wanted to beat her until I didn't love her anymore, but that was proving to be impossible.

"I loved you, shorty, and I was good to you. How the fuck could you do me like this?" I frowned, feeling tears well up. As soon as I felt a lone tear hit the top of my lip, I quickly wiped it away.

"I'm sorry," she cried with her eyes closed. Her face was covered in blood, and she was balled up like some wounded animal. "I'm sorry!"

"I'm killing his ass!"

"No! Don't!" she had the nerve to holler, stopping me in my tracks.

"Oh damn. What, you love this nigga?" my breathing became even heavier as my fists continued to open and close. How dare she beg for me not to hurt him after she cheated on me with him? "Answer me!" I snatched her up by her hair.

"Yes! I love him! I loved him before I even met you! But it's over now, he doesn't want me!"

I wanted to kill her but I couldn't. I loved the hoe, and would be hurting myself more if I put a bullet in her. I was about to knock her ass across the face again when I heard someone coming into the house.

"Hayden—"

POP!

I drew my gun and fired a bullet before I could even really see who it was.

"Nooooo!!!!!" Hayden screamed once Ingrid dropped to the floor. She was dead already since I put the bullet between her eyes. "Ingrid!" Hayden climbed out of the tub and raced over to her.

"Baby, I didn't know it was—" I tried to touch her.

"Get off me!" she cried and hugged Ingrid's head into her chest, not caring that blood was getting all over her clothes. "Get out!"

Stepping over them, I just grabbed my food and left. It's crazy how life could go from sugar to shit in a matter of minutes.

Goldie Taylor

I'd just come from an interview to be an intern for this fashion magazine, and they hired me on the spot. For a while now, I'd been upset because of what had happened to Kimberlyn, but this really improved my spirits. I hoped to stick with the company and become a fashion editor. That had been my dream job for the longest, so to say that this opportunity was exciting would be an understatement. Not only would I be compensated, but I would get college credits and bonus points with the company.

I decided to treat myself to some Tasty Burger, and I even planned to eat there. The employee who saw me fight Juanita seemed to be over the situation, so she didn't give me any problems when I came in. I was happy about that because I loved this place.

I ordered my food, and then sat down to wait for my number to be called. As I was scrolling through Instagram, someone came and sat across from me. I was praying that it wasn't another bitch of Ethan's, or someone coming to knock me across the dome like they'd done Kimberlyn. I was starting to realize that the Quinton boys were not worth the hassle. Summer got shot, Kimberlyn was bludgeoned, I got jumped, and now we were just waiting to see what havoc Lendsey would cause Matikah. I'm sure it didn't matter that they were broken up.

I looked up slowly to see sexy ass Britain smirking at me. I hadn't talked to him since I fought his girlfriend, and I had no plans on doing so. Yeah, I missed the sex and conversation, but I wasn't looking to be anyone's side chick. The friends with benefits idea was cool in the beginning, but I refused to do something that I wouldn't want done to me. If I were in Tekeya's place, I would've snatched my ass up out the car too. I wouldn't have lost that fight though.

"What?" I sucked my teeth.

"I like when you get an attitude, it makes me want to fuck that shit up out of you," he licked his full lips, making my pussy salivate. I missed his head game.

"Can you leave me alone before your girl pops up again? If I have to fight again, I'm coming for your ass next."

He got up and came around the table to sit next to me.

"Don't be like that, Goldie. You know who I wanna be with, shorty." He kissed on my neck, and rubbed between my legs with his big, strong hand.

"Stop, Britain," I moaned as he began sucking on my neck ever so gently.

"I missed you, G."

"Number forty-four!" the clerk yelled, snapping me out of my trance. Pushing Britain's hand from between my legs, I hopped up to grab my food.

I wished I hadn't told her it was for here, because she handed me a tray with the food all out in the open. I walked back over and sat down next to him, inhaling his Jo Malone London cologne. That shit smelled so good, and now sometimes when I went to department stores, I would smell it just to remember him.

He ate one of my fries, making me chuckle. He then resumed kissing my cheek and then my neck, before caressing my leg. I just continued to eat like it was nothing, trying to ignore him. I was so wet at the moment, but I refused to go home with him and let him fuck me.

"Come with me when you finish your food," he said.

"No Britain, damn. Go find Tekeya!" I snapped and bit my burger.

"I know where she is already, but I want to be around you. You've been ignoring me for weeks now, shorty. Damn, when are you gonna forgive me?"

"That's the thing, homie, I don't plan on forgiving your ass at all. You told me we were gonna be friends with benefits, but then you get mad when I talk to other guys. Then because you were in your feelings, we got caught and I had to fight."

"I know, aight? I don't need a fucking recap. I can't help the fact that I don't like other niggas fucking you."

"I told you I wasn't fucking anyone else, but I should be able to do so if I want. Just like you can go fuck Tekeya and any other bitch you want."

"So you're telling me you wouldn't mind if I smashed some other girl outside of Key?" he pursed his lips, making him look way too fucking fine for words. *God, give me the strength,* I silently prayed.

"I don't want you fucking anyone, not even Tekeya, but that was what we agreed to so I can't get upset. See, I understand that, you're the only one who doesn't."

"I'm stingy with my pussy, especially when it's as good as yours," he whispered onto my neck, sending one thousand chills down my spine. "I miss you and I haven't felt you in a long time. I'm dying." He kissed the corner of my mouth, and then turned me to face him before pecking me.

His soft lips were sent from heaven, and soon enough our tongues were doing the mambo. I loved kissing him, and deep down I wanted to be his girl. I knew that would never happen though, which is why I planned to cut him off. I was doing okay, despite him bothering me all day and night, but right now he had me feeling weak in the knees like SWV.

"Move, Britain," I nudged him back, since the kiss was feeling way better than it should have. He tried to force his lips on me again, but I mushed his face. "Move, you need to go be with your girlfriend." I stood up.

"I want you, though."

"Well, that's too bad, Britain. You set rules that you can't even follow." I began gathering my food so that I could get a bag from the front.

"Goldie!" he called after me as I walked to the counter to get a bag. As I was doing so, he got up to approach me, but two girls blocked his pathway, being thirsty.

I just chuckled as I packed my food up. I continued out as he attempted to get past the girls.

"Goldie!"

"What?"

"I'm gonna FaceTime you tonight, and you better answer."

"Boy, bye!" is what I said, but I was praying in my head that I fell asleep, or was just strong enough to continue to ignore him.

CHAPTER TWO

Lendsey Quinton

One week later…

All up in my face, you not from the clique. Give me space, we might rob the shit. Most hate it, baby they don't love the clique. I thought they love you when you make it. This some other shit, yeah…

Tonight my brothers and I were out to have a little bit of fun. We rarely went to clubs that were open to the public, but every now and then we wanted to let loose and not have to throw our own shit. Girls were all over our VIP shaking their asses to "Why You Always Hatin'?" by YG. A lot of them looked good as hell, but only one shorty was on my mind. Too bad she wasn't paying me any attention.

"Aye, is Kimberlyn coming?" I quizzed TQ as he sipped his Jack Daniels.

"Nah, I told you she was too sick," he replied.

"Again? Nigga, she's been too sick for the last couple of days," I frowned. "You need to take her ass back to the hospital."

"She good, aight?"

Britain, Rhys, and I all looked at one another, and then back to TQ's weird ass. He was bobbing his head, flashing a few smiles at the sexy shorties up here with us.

"You got her pregnant, didn't you?" Rhys quizzed, saying what was on our minds.

"What the fuck did I tell y'all about worrying about what I got going on? If you see a baby in nine or something months, you will have an answer."

"I already got my answer," Britain responded as he refilled his glass.

"Anyway, none of the ladies from that circle are coming?" I questioned. I really wanted to see Matikah, and I knew this might be the only way. She had me acting weird as fuck, and I didn't like it.

"I texted Goldie and invited her, so who knows," Britain shrugged.

"Hey, daddy," Dania appeared. "They let me up because they recognized me. Want a lap dance?" she smiled. I hadn't seen Dania in a while, and damn, I almost forgot how damn good her ass looked.

"Yeah, go ahead," I sighed. Fuck it, Matikah wouldn't care anyways. Plus, she wasn't even gonna be here tonight.

"Energy" by Drake was playing over the club at the moment, and Dania was moving her body in my lap perfectly. She wasn't dancing long, before my neglected ass dick sprang up. I hadn't gotten any play since Matikah left a nigga, and I think it was about time that I ended that damn drought.

"Come on," I whispered into her ear and tapped the side of her thigh lightly.

"Where are we going?" she looked over her shoulder.

"Bathroom."

We both got up, and I took her hand into mine to lead her to the back. Some chick tried to come along, but I wasn't in the mood for all that. I just wanted to bust this nut so I wouldn't be so damn backed up. I couldn't believe Matikah had me out here being a bitch and turning my back on my needs.

As soon as we got into the bathroom, I locked the door and began pushing her dress up her smooth thighs. She wanted to kiss, but I wasn't in the mood for that shit; I wanted to fuck. Placing a few kisses on her neck, I ripped her panties off and threw them over my shoulder.

"I love when you get like this, Len," she moaned, as I ran my fingers across her clit.

I turned her around, and bent her over the sink before releasing the beast. I quickly ripped open a condom from my wallet, rolled it down, and then slid inside of her. Her walls were pulling me in like a muthafucka, and I had to brace myself. Her pussy was on that vacuum shit.

"Shit," I grumbled.

"Oooh, oooh, fuck, Len!" she cried out as I pummeled her pussy from the back. This shit was so damn good that I almost wanted to holler out too.

Seeing her ass jiggling and shit was all I needed to send me over the edge, but I held out a little longer. She gushed on my pole, and that was it, I busted. I panted heavily for a bit, and then slid out of her. I flushed the condom, and then grabbed some paper towels to wet with water and soap to clean myself. She used some little wipes she had in her purse, and then we both washed our hands. As I buckled my jeans, she sprayed herself with a few spritz of perfume, before turning to me and draping her arms over my shoulders.

"What happened to the baby you were supposedly pregnant with?" I asked. She hadn't mentioned the damn baby since the day I let her ruin my life.

"False alarm," she shrugged.

"Right."

We exited the bathroom, and Dania hugged me from behind as we got closer to where I was originally seated with my brothers. I usually didn't like displaying affection like this with her, but I was slightly tipsy, happy I busted a nut, and not in the mood to see her pout and moan when I moved her hands. I quickly regretted my decision when I saw that Goldie and Matikah decided to show up.

Britain was all in Goldie's face, a little ways from the VIP crowd, but Matikah was chilling by Rhys, making herself a drink. I tried to quickly remove Dania's hands from my waist, but Matikah had already seen everything. Fuck!

"Hey, shorty," I said before sitting down.

"Hello," she replied dryly as Dania sat in my lap.

"Move, ma," I said in a low tone as I took her out of my lap to place her next to me.

"Oh, now you want me to move because you got some pussy, right?" Dania spat before sitting back and folding her arms across her breasts. I knew she was being extra because of Matikah.

Rhys shook his head at me while lighting his blunt. Matikah just chuckled and got up with her drink to go dance by the balcony of the club. Dropping my head, I massaged my temples to ease the sudden headache. It seemed like no matter what happened, I would never be able to get Matikah back. It was no one's fault but mine though.

Summer Gillies

"Mommy, when are we going back home where daddy is?" Bryleigh asked me in the car. We were on our way to my mother's house so I could drop her off. My mother would then take her to her preschool when it was time.

"You don't like where we live now?"

We'd just moved from staying with my mom, to a condo out in Allston, about fifteen minutes from the old condo that we lived in with Rhys. I enjoyed being on my own, and because Rhys barely slept in the bed with me, I didn't miss cuddling or anything like that. Strangely enough, knowing he wouldn't be coming in randomly, bothered me a little bit, but not enough to take him back.

I told him if he ever cheated on me again that it was over, and I guess he thought I was joking. It took so damn much out of me to decide to leave him. The whole way home after seeing that picture message of him and Chenaye, I was trying to tell myself every excuse in the world so that I would have a reason to stay. I had to just grow some balls and realize that Rhys would never change for me, and despite what he said, he was just like his hoe ass brothers.

I made it to my mother's home in East Boston, and parked right out front. Unbuckling Bryleigh, I grabbed her little backpack and lunch, before we headed up the stairs and into the house.

"Hey, baby," my mother greeted me and then picked up Bryleigh. "Want some breakfast?" she asked us both.

"Yes, please!" Bryleigh giggled.

"Oh, I have to be at work—"

"No, please stay with us, Mommy!"

I stared into my daughter's little cute face for a bit, and then smiled. She could always get her way with Rhys and I, because she was so cute and such a good little girl. It was hard to say no to a child that was so well behaved and intelligent.

"Okay, fine. What did you make?" I questioned my mom as I followed her into the kitchen.

"I made your favorite, a breakfast scramble." She sat Bryleigh at the table as I sat down in a chair as well. She piled some of the scramble onto our plates, and then brought us a glass of orange juice before fixing her own dish.

"Thanks, Ma. What do you say, Bry?"

"Thank you!" she poked her little lips out before sipping her juice.

"She is a perfect mixture of you and Rhys," my mother smiled at her. "Why don't you go eat in the living room? I can turn the TV on for you," my mom offered Bryleigh.

"Yay!!!" she squealed and rushed off to the living room. I chuckled as my mother carried Bryleigh's food and juice to the living room to set her up.

"So, what's going on with you and Rhys, Summer?" She returned and sat back down to eat.

"Nothing, why do you ask?"

"I'm asking because you refuse to see him. You're making him pick Bry up from me or his parents, instead of meeting in person like you guys used to do."

"Used to do? You're making it sound like we've been separated for years or something. It's only been about a month, Ma, and I just feel it's best, the less we see of one another."

"For who?"

"Huh?"

"Best for whom?"

"Best for the three of us; me, him, and Bryleigh."

"No, I think you're avoiding him for some reason, Summer. The look on his face when he picks her up from me tells me that he's hoping he runs into you."

"Well, he should've thought about that before he decided to cheat on me with some hood rat named Chenaye." I stabbed my food. "Or maybe before one of his side chicks shot me."

I still to this day couldn't believe that shit. That was definitely God trying to tell me to leave his ass alone.

"I agree. I just think that you need to be more cordial to one another since you share a child." I was about to speak, but instead, tears began spilling down my cheeks. "Summer, honey, calm down." My mother got up and came around to hug me.

"I miss him, Ma, and I shouldn't! I've been praying every morning and night to be over him, and it hasn't worked. It seems to be doing the opposite," I sobbed hysterically. My mom rubbed my head, but then let me go to close the kitchen divider, before returning to sit next to me.

"I didn't want Bry and your father to hear. You know your dad is crazy and will be ready to kill if he sees you crying," she half smiled. "Honey, I know it's hard to move on, but you have to realize that you're wasting your precious life trying to be with a man who will never love you the way you wanna be loved."

"You don't think he's capable?" I sniffled.

"I think he is, all men are, its just that it takes a certain woman to bring it out of them. It's hard to tell yourself that you aren't the one, because we all want to be the girl that gets him to change."

She was right. It hurt like hell to realize that I wasn't good enough to change Rhys, and that some other woman would be the one to make him become a better man. It made me wonder what was wrong with me.

"I hate this," I whispered.

"I know, and I hate to see you like this. But understand that you are the one for somebody, just not Rhys Quinton."

The sound of his name made me queasy, that's how much I loved him. Whenever he was mentioned, my stomach would drop and my palms would sweat. It was as if I was terrified to hear something about him that I didn't want to.

"I have to get to work, Ma." I stood up and polished off my juice. She got up to hug me tightly, and then I left out after kissing Bryleigh and speaking to my father.

I had to be stronger and get over this nigga, otherwise I would never be happy.

Kimberlyn Harrey

I was in my school's library doing some homework and stressing. I was in school studying art design, because I wanted to be a website designer. I loved my classes that weren't general education, but being pregnant while trying to focus on HTML codes and shit, was not the business. All I wanted to do these days, was eat snacks, watch TV, and pray that I wouldn't throw up as violently as the morning before.

After completing a couple more web tabs, I decided I would go to TQ's house so that I could take a nice hot bath in his tub, cook us some food, and hopefully refresh my mind enough to continue some more work.

I made it out into the parking lot, and saw a big black truck that I recognized all too well. I hoped he wasn't here for me, because I just didn't want those damn problems at the moment. I'd never witnessed TQ's wrath, and frankly I'd like to keep it that way.

"Kimberlyn, got these for you." Gang hopped out the back seat of the all black Chevy Suburban, and handed me a big huge bouquet of yellow roses.

"Thank you," I said in a low tone, before hesitantly taking them. "Gang, you—"

"I know, I shouldn't be talking to you, which is why I decided to come up to your school instead of your house. I know your boy has eyes on you all around Roxbury, but I figured around here we were safe." I didn't say anything because I had nothing to say, so he continued. "Can we go to the food court, I just want to talk, Kimberlyn?"

"Gang, I told you—"

"Just think, Kimberlyn, we used to be really cool. You're telling me that you want to be with a man who would put restrictions on you like that? Look, I respect your relationship with him now, and I just want to catch up, as friends. We used to have some fun together, remember?" he smiled with his adorable self.

He was right, we did used to be good friends, but I was still worried about TQ's people seeing me with him. I knew Gang doubted that TQ had eyes everywhere, but I didn't. However, I was my own person and since Gang understood that he and I would never be, I saw no harm in having a platonic conversation and friendship with him.

"Okay, I will give you thirty minutes, but after that I have to go home," I smiled and so did he.

"More than enough time."

We made it to the student union, and found an empty table to sit at. I waited as he purchased some snacks, before coming to sit down across from me.

"So what's new?" I asked, not knowing how to start this catching up conversation.

"Nothing much, just been working and stuff. I was off my game for a bit, so it feels good to finally get back to normal, or at least *almost* back to normal."

"Why were you off your game?" I sipped my water.

"Honestly?"

"Umm yeah, honestly. I don't want you to lie."

"Because of you. I was losing my mind not talking to you, and knowing that you had moved on to someone I knew."

"Oh, that."

"Yeah, and can I tell you something? I need it stay between you and I, don't even tell Matikah, Goldie, or nothing like that."

"You can tell me. I will keep it between us."

"Cool. I was off my game not only because we weren't building anymore, but because you chose someone who I felt wasn't good for you, shorty."

"I disagree. I think TQ is perfect for me."

"Really? I thought you liked the one-woman man type, that's definitely not TQ. I mean, just recently Peel found out he was smashing Hayden."

"I knew that already, Gang, and that's been over for some time."

"Nah, it hasn't. They just broke things off because Peel caught her crying about it, when before she seemed to be all good."

My heart rate began to speed up as I processed what Gang was telling me. I was so in love with TQ that I couldn't believe what he was saying to me. The man I had grown to know, loved me, and would never be cheating on me in this stage of our relationship. Maybe love was blinding me, but my brain just wouldn't believe it.

"Doubt it," I half smiled.

"You love him?" he asked and I nodded slowly. "Did you ever love me?"

"I—"

Suddenly my phone chimed, and it was a notification from one of my many pregnancy apps. Gang snatched my iPhone up with the quickness, and stared at it longer than he needed to. You would think it was a book on my lock screen because of how long he took.

"You're trying to get pregnant?" He turned my phone to me so that I could see.

"Gang, no, I—"

"You already are. Damn," he paused as if he were paralyzed, and searched my eyes with his. If I didn't know any better, I would think he was about to cry. "A baby, Kimberlyn?" he looked deeper into my eyes, and I did see that his were a bit glazed over. The notorious Gang was broken up? This would be a day for the history books.

"We didn't plan anything, Gang, it just… things just happen for a reason, okay?" I stood up and grabbed my phone and books. "See you later," I rushed off. I checked over my shoulder once more, and he was still sitting there staring down at the table. I hadn't realized how much of an impression I'd made on the nigga.

I made it to TQ's condo, and couldn't get inside to pee fast enough. I relived myself, and then came out to see TQ sitting on the couch, quietly sipping a dark drink. He must've just gotten here, because he wasn't sitting there when I came in. He looked just as handsome as always, but I could see his strong jaw clenching, which meant he was angry.

"Hi baby, I'm gonna make chicken nachos tonight like you asked," I chuckled lightly as I neared him slowly.

"Fuck did I tell you, Kimberlyn?"

"Huh?"

"What. The. Fuck. Did. I. Tell. You," he stated, making every word sound like one separate sentence.

"About the nachos?" I played dumb.

"About Gang!!" he roared and shot up off the couch, prompting me to stumble back in fear. Fire burned inside of his deep blue gray eyes, and his caramel complexion looked as if it were on fire.

"You said—"

"I said to not spend any fucking time with him! I said to cease all muthafuckin contact with that bitch ass nigga, didn't I?" He swung his glass of liquor and ice around. I just stared so he yelled, "Didn't I?!"

"Yes!"

"I'm sure you thought I didn't have eyes at your school, and you're right, I didn't. But I know people, and someone got a couple photos of you for me, accepting flowers and having conversation." He neared me wearing the most evil yet sexy grin I'd ever seen.

"I know, but—"

"Where are the damn flowers?" He kept moving near me, and I kept moving away from his tall, angry ass.

"I left them on accident. I mean, I left them on purpose!"

"Stay the fuck away from Gang, Kimberlyn, and I mean it!" He slammed his hand into the wall we were up against. "One more fucking time, and we're gonna have some damn problems! I should go blow his fucking head open right now!"

"No, Tarenz—" I stopped when he raised both eyebrows as if he were surprised.

"Okay, I won't kill him. I will let him live so y'all can be together. That's what you want, right?"

"No I don't, I just don't want you to kill him for nothing. We were just talking, Tarenz, and why can't we be friends? It's not like we've had sex before or anything."

"You're right," he backed away with a closed mouth smile. "Have sex all y'all want now, I'm done with this shit, Kimberlyn." He grabbed his jacket as I began to sob.

He stormed to the door, but stopped when I shouted through an abundance of tears, "What about the baby?"

He stood there silent with his back to me, before closing the door back. He hung his jacket back up, and then walked over to me. By now I was sitting on the floor crying my eyes out. Everything had just happened so fast, and it was like I had no way of stopping it.

Sighing heavily, he scooped me and walked me over to the couch after kissing my cheek. We sat down with me in his lap, and without any words, we just hugged one another tightly. I caressed the back of his head as he kissed my neck lightly.

"Stop crying, shorty, I'm sorry. I've never been jealous in my life, so I didn't know what to say or do," he whispered. "I just love you so much."

Hearing his last sentence made my heart melt. I could tell he meant it, and that gave me a warm sensation all over my body.

"I love you too, and I'm sorry. I won't entertain him anymore." I held his face in my hands. He nodded before we engaged in a passionate kiss.

What the fuck just happened?

Britain Quinton

I was at Quinton Car Wash going over the books, and since I'd finished early, I wanted to check on some of the loans my dad had given out. I knew a couple people were nearing that past due mark, and one in particular hadn't contacted me at all.

A friend of my father's named Danil Smirnov, was this Russian gangster who moved from Russia illegally, like my father, and made a home in New York. He assisted my father here and there with little shit whenever he needed to get paid, but he wasn't an official member of QCF if you will. This nigga stayed borrowing cash from my father, and this last time, he'd borrowed one hundred thousand dollars in which he was supposed to make five payments of twenty grand.

See, Mr. Smirnov was a heavy gambler, and in the days when he and my dad would occasionally run together, he made a lot of money. My father told me that Mr. Smirnov had made about ten million dollars in just two years, from illegal gambling and fixing sports games. These days, he was losing left and right, and borrowing every time he did. And with every loan request, he would always tell my dad that he was sure he would win double whatever he borrowed. If it were up to me, I would have been cut the nigga off, but my dad had love for his ass, so he continued to put faith in the nigga. I admit I felt sorry for him, but not enough to agree with my father on loaning him huge amounts.

I dialed Mr. Smirnov on my burner phone, and waited as the line trilled. *This nigga better pick up*, I thought.

"Zdravstvuyte? (Hello?)" he answered in Russian.

"Ey, my mozhem govorit' po-angliyski? (Hey, can we speak English?)," I quizzed, before getting started.

"Britain? Konechno, (Britain? Sure)," he sighed.

"Spasibo. (Thanks). Mr. Smirnov, I'm calling because you're three months behind with your payments. You've paid only twenty-thousand, and we gave you an extension for the month after that, but now it's been two more months and it's forty grand due."

"I see. I spoke with your father and he told me that everything is okay."

"No, you didn't speak with my father, and if you did, he wouldn't have said it was okay, Mr. Smirnov. I handle my father's loans, so there would be no reason for you to call him. And if you did, he would direct you to me."

"Everyone else, yes, but your father and I are, how do you say umm, khoroshiye druz'ya (good friends)," he explained.

"Business is business, Mr. Smirnov. My father does not change the rules depending on the person. Now I agree he has been very lenient with you, considering the fact that we don't usually do payment plans, but we need the forty grand to bring you current. When can I get it?"

"Ya budu govorit' s Stony eh? (I will speak with Stony)."

"No, no you won't. Have the forty grand ready in one damn week or I will be forced to take action, and neither one of us wants that, Mr.

Smirnov."

"Konechno, syn (Sure, son)," he chuckled and disconnected.

Mr. Smirnov felt that my dad protected him from me, and that couldn't be further from the truth. I had a job to do, and since he didn't want to adhere to the rules and regulations, I would be visiting New York very soon.

I looked at my personal phone, and smiled when I thought about Goldie. The day that I'd seen her at Tasty's, I called her on FaceTime that night and little mama answered. As soon as her pretty face came on that screen, my dick was trying to get in the camera and ask her where she'd been. I wanted Goldie to be my girlfriend, and I wasn't afraid to admit it.

Picking up my phone, I went to our old ass text conversation and began typing.

***Me:** What are you doing?*

***Baby Mama:** Minding my business…*

I chuckled because I could hear that in her voice, and picture her rolling her eyes.

***Me:** You only have classes on Monday and Wednesday right?*

***Baby Mama:** Yes, stalking ass nigga lol.*

***Me:** Come with me to NY on Thursday, we will come back Sunday.*

***Baby Mama:** Is your girlfriend coming too?*

***Me:** I don't have a girlfriend anymore, so are you down?*

I wasn't being all the way truthful. I mean, Tekeya was still technically my girlfriend because we hadn't officially said those words, but we hadn't talked much since the park/party incident. I was hoping shit would just dwindle until there was nothing left. The thought of talking to her made me shudder, because I knew it would end with a tussle.

Baby Mama: *Fine, but I'm not paying for shit nor will I be letting you fuck.*

Me: *Wouldn't expect you to pay anything, and umm, right.*

I got hard just thinking about smashing.

Suddenly, my phone flew from my hands onto the floor. I looked up to see a fuming Tekeya, as I picked it up, locked it, and placed it on the desk. *Why did I leave the office door open?*

"So you do me dirty and then don't say shit, nigga?" she spat, folding her arms across her big breasts.

"Key, what do you want me to say? You caught me red handed, I really don't know what to say to you, ma."

I was still a little peeved about her knocking my fucking phone out my hand. She cracked the last one, and although richer than a muthafucka, I wasn't trying to be dropping another grand for a new iPhone.

"You need to be begging me!" she screamed and began to cry. Here we fucking go with this shit, man.

"Key, maybe it's best we be apart. I mean, shit ain't working out like it used to, and we're both unhappy." I stood up.

"I am happy, Britain."

"How?" I sat on the edge of the desk. "How are you happy when we argue constantly, we barely spend time together, and we haven't even had sex in about a month and a half?" I was really confused.

"Because you've been too busy sticking your dick in other bitches!!" she screeched and began taking off on me.

"Bitch ass nigga!" Her home girl, Angelica, came rushing in and joined her in hitting me everywhere they could reach. Was I really getting jumped?

"Back the fuck up, Key!" I barked, grabbing her wrists and shaking her. Angelica stopped wailing on me once I got Tekeya off; I guess she wasn't shit without her.

"Get off me!" Tekeya screamed.

"I'm calling the police!" Angelica slipped out of the office.

I let go of Tekeya to chase her, but Tekeya began raining blows on me before I could even get around her. I grabbed her wrists again, and tried to calm her down. True to her routine, she was now crying and hollering like she was so upset.

"Key, shorty, please calm down. This is exactly why I don't want this anymore. If you're happy then I don't know what to say, but I am miserable. I can't do this shit anymore."

We were both breathing heavily, except she was crying her eyes out. I felt bad, but not too much, because she always did this shit. There was never talking with Tekeya. She always wanted to use her fists. If I were a different type of nigga, I would have been knocked her little ass the fuck out.

My phone chimed, and we both looked down at it.

"Baby mama? Nigga, you got a baby?" she growled as if she were some pit bull.

"Tekeya—"

She was right back to throwing them hands, and we were moving all around the office like some ignoramus'. Papers were flying everywhere, but when I heard my phone fall and make a sound as if it had cracked, I lost it. Gripping her by the neck, I placed her against the wall while panting angrily.

"I told you to—"

"Put her down!" I looked to see who was yelling, and couldn't believe that bitch Angelica had for real called the police on me. "Put her down, or I will be forced to shoot," the officer grimaced.

I let go of her neck, and put my hands up in mock surrender. I couldn't believe this shit. Tekeya ran and hid behind the officer like she wasn't just whooping my ass five minutes ago. I wasn't even choking the bitch, I just had my hand around her dramatic ass neck.

"What the fuck!" I shouted once the officer began cuffing me.

Tekeya and Angelica were wearing smug expressions as the policeman walked me out of the office in handcuffs. All the car wash customers and employees were staring at me, mouths ajar. I just sighed and kept my mouth shut even though I wanted to go the fuck off.

"I'll take him, Allen," one officer walked up, talking to the officer who'd cuffed me.

"You sure?"

"Yeah, I'm sure."

The new officer grabbed my arm and led me to his patrol car, before placing me in the back seat. As I sat back there, I watched Angelica and Tekeya speed out of the car wash with Nicki Minaj blasting as if life was good.

The new officer, who requested to take me, finally got into the driver's seat and pulled off. It was quiet for a few moments, but I saw that he kept glancing at me through the rearview mirror.

"Britain Quinton?" he finally asked.

"Yeah, man," I responded somberly as I looked out of the window.

"I'm sorry about that back there. Let me just make a stop at Starbucks, and then I will take you back to the car wash."

"Huh?"

"Your dad, Stony, has me on payroll. I'm sure he will soon have Allen on as well, but he's new so he doesn't know that you guys are off limits yet."

"I see. Well just hurry up with the Starbucks please, I need to lock up the office and get my car," I sighed.

"Sure thing, boss."

I was happy that the Quinton name meant so much, not just here in Boston, but the whole East Coast. However, I was angry that Tekeya had gone this far. I was done with that bitch, and that's on everything I love.

CHAPTER THREE

Matikah

The next night...

Tonight, Summer and I were gonna go out and have a little girls' night. Goldie said she had some work to do for her new internship, and Kimberlyn said she was behind on her schoolwork so they couldn't come. I was bummed that they had declined my invitation, but when Summer agreed, I was back to being excited.

Summer and I have never hung together alone, but I was looking forward to it. She had a genuine personality and I liked that. I think we also could bond over the fact that we had scars on our hearts from those stupid ass Quintons.

The club was located on Warrenton Street, and it was pretty popular. Only people who had money, dressed nice, or were about something went to this club. In fact, I'd come to an event with Lendsey here before. Seeing the venue again gave me a sharp pain in my heart, because it reminded me of all the good times Lendsey and I had.

"Ready?" Summer smiled as we exited the Uber.

"Yes, but damn, look at this line." The line was all the way down Warrenton, wrapping around and hitting Charles Street.

"I know. But I've been with Rhys for so long that sometimes I get the same privileges as him. They know me here, and I'm sure they will have no problem letting us in."

I nodded and followed Summer up to the front where the two big ass bouncers were. I prayed that we got in, because how stupid would we look walking up to the front like we were about something, just to get turned away.

"Summer, what's up, baby girl?" one bouncer smiled and hugged her lightly. Thank God.

"Hey Sean, me and my friend, Matikah, wanna party, can you let us in?" she asked sweetly, tossing her long, beautiful dreads to the other side.

"I can get you in, no problem, but I'm not sure I have a table that's free for you," he sighed and looked at a sheet of paper attached to his clipboard.

"Oh, it's fine. I will just call Rhys and tell him that we can get in, just no table."

"Wait, wait, let me double check before you do all that, ma," he chuckled lightly, almost as if hearing Rhys' named frightened him. He spoke into his radio for a couple moments, and then finally put the small black device away. "Turns out I have something for you, Summer, just give me a few moments."

She nodded in response, and we stood there smiling at one another while waiting. Suddenly, we heard some girls yelling obscenities.

"Back up a bit," Sean told us.

Next thing I knew, three girls were being brought out of the club and manhandled while shouting. They were obviously a little tipsy, but still coherent enough to be angry. By what they were hollering, I could tell that we'd gotten their table. I felt kind of bad, but not bad enough to turn down the table. A few more moments passed, and we were led up to the VIP section, which I could tell had been cleaned, refreshed, and restocked.

"Enjoy, ladies," the female bouncer smiled and pranced out.

"Good thing he didn't allow you to call Rhys, huh?" I chuckled as I opened the bottle of liquor.

"And if he did, Rhys would have still got him straight. My baby daddy still loves me, we just can't be together," she responded and held her glass out to me.

"So you would never get back with him?" I filled her glass with juice and vodka.

"No, I can't. You know sometimes I have the urge to be with him again, but I have to remind myself that I deserve better."

"Yeah," I nodded and sipped my drink.

I knew all too well what she meant. I missed Lendsey more and more everyday, but I knew he was no good. The night I saw him walking up with Dania hugging him, I almost threw up because that's how sick it made me. After the club, I cried for a long ass time in the shower. My grandmother thought I'd drowned because I was in there for so long. All this time I thought he really wanted to be with me, but seeing him with Dania that night let me know that I wasn't that important to him. Thinking about it made my eyes water, so I quickly took my drink to the head and refilled it.

"Damn, you're ready to party, huh?" Summer chuckled at me.

"Yes I am. We need to have some fun and quit sulking!"

I stood up and began dancing to "Look Alive" by Rae Sremmurd. Summer got up to join me, and once the liquor started taking effect, I was having the time of my life. As I moved to "Nothing is Promised" by Mike Will Made It, I felt someone hug me from behind. It was odd for someone to be granted access to our VIP, but I was too twisted to care. I brought my hands to place on top of his, and I recognized the feeling. Those hands had touched me all over, done all kinds of things to me, and I would never forget them.

I turned around to face Lendsey, and before I could say anything, he was kissing me roughly. It felt so good, and in combination with me being drunk and the loud music, I was all into it. I usually would've slapped the shit out of him, but I instead hugged his torso tightly. He was holding my face, and you could tell how much we missed one another by the way we kissed. Our tongues were entangled, and our lips were pressing together hard as fuck, as if we were trying to become one.

"I missed you," he whispered.

"Show me how much," I responded out of being tipsy and in love.

He took my hand into his, and led me to the back of the VIP, up some stairs, and into this private room where there was a big red velvet couch. I didn't know why this room was here since it wasn't a strip club or anything. Closing the door, he pulled me into him and we resumed kissing. We'd knocked a couple things over but we didn't care. In a matter of seconds, my dress was up, my panties were off, and his dick was out. Pressing me against the wall, he held my legs apart before entering me slowly. He was struggling a little bit since he hadn't touched me in months, but he was hard enough to make it inside soon enough.

The feeling of his big dick entering me, was painful yet pleasurable at the same time. We kept on kissing as he thrust into me, making me tremble and cry out as if I were being killed. It should've been a sin for him to make me feel this way.

"I love you, Lendsey," I moaned and gripped his kinky hair.

"Shit, you better not have given my pussy away. Fuck," he groaned. Hearing him moan and groan got me even wetter, and now the sound of him going in and out of me seemed to be loud as hell. "I love you, Tikah. Baby, I'm sorry," he continued as he pumped me with precision.

"Mmm, uuuh, uuuh, uuuh!" we hollered out together before we both exploded.

Panting heavily, we resumed kissing like maniacs, until he finally pulled out of me and let me down. Although still drunk, my guilty conscience began to rear its ugly head. What had I done? This man broke my heart and I allowed him to come in here and sleep with me like some hoe. He did it to me just how he did it with Dania, who was pregnant by him.

"I can drive you home," he smiled as he fixed himself.

"No, Lendsey, this was a mistake." I opened the door to leave.

"What? No, Matikah, this was not a mistake." He slammed the door back closed. "Baby, I'm sorry, I don't know what else to say or do. I got you flowers, gifts, I've pleaded my case, I even had my mama call you. What more do you want?"

"I want you to leave me alone, Lendsey. I can't even look at you without feeling like crying. I don't know why I let you do what you just did—"

"Because I love you and you love me," he kissed my lips, the corner of my mouth, and then began sucking on my neck perfectly.

"You love me but you did the same thing we just did with Dania." I nudged him off once I realized him sucking on my neck was getting me horny again."

"Man, *we* just made love. I fucked Dania because it was convenient. I just slept with you because I miss you, baby, and I need you back in my life." He pecked my lips gently and repeatedly.

"Move, Lendsey," I sobbed, as he kissed all over my face, neck, and shoulders, while groping my ass.

"Matikah—"

"Move! It's over with!" I kneed him in the nuts and scurried out as he yowled in pain. "Summer, order the Uber so we can leave."

"What? Where is Lendsey?"

"I don't know and I don't care, come on." We rushed out of the VIP and down the steps as she ordered the Uber car.

I was so disappointed in myself.

Rhys Quinton

The next evening…

"Rhys, I need a favor," my sister Saya pleaded as soon as I answered the fucking phone.

"And hello to yo' ass too!"

"Hi, but I don't have time for the formalities, this is an emergency, bro."

"What?" I asked before taking a big pull on the blunt I was smoking.

This weed I'd gotten was strong as fuck and had me on one. All I did was smoke weed these days, unless I had my daughter with me. Whenever I was supposed to pick her up or have her for the weekend, I stayed sober. But when a nigga was by himself, I got so high sometimes I thought I would be able to levitate.

"I need you to go to the Mandarin Oriental."

"The hotel? For what, Saya?" I frowned and sat up. This was some straight bullshit. I wasn't in the mood to do anything but sit here and figure out ways I could get Summer back.

"One of the girls is a little uncomfortable with her john, and they're meeting later at that hotel. I need you to be there in case something happens to her. They will be staying in the dynasty suite, and I already told the clerk at the front desk to have a key for you."

"Fuck am I supposed to do, Saya? Sit in the closet like some hoe and watch her fuck this nigga? What, she wants me to make sure he don't nut in her mouth?"

"Stop being disrespectful, Rhys. You know our girls are not some Las Vegas strip walkers, they have class. Now just do what you do, and make sure he doesn't touch her when she doesn't want to be touched. Then once everything is settled, find a way to sneak out. You need to leave now, bro, because they will be arriving in thirty minutes."

"My regular fee for this, whether I have to kill him or not."

"I know. Mom has your one hundred grand ready and waiting. I will tell her that you want payment even if you don't have to kill him."

"Bye, Saya."

"Thank you, Rhys, I love you!" she squealed. I just disconnected while sighing. Soon after, she texted some details to my burner number.

I changed into some all black jeans, a black t-shirt, black hoodie, and some all black Nike Air Force. Once I was good to go, I grabbed some heat and left. I made it to the hotel, which was located on Boylston Street, and parked around the back. In case I did have to murk this nigga, I wanted to be able to slip out of here discreetly, and having to wait for valet wasn't exactly my idea of being subtle.

Making my way inside the hotel, I went to the front desk and requested a key to the room from a specific clerk, as Saya had instructed. Like she said, there was a key waiting for me, so there was no hassle. All

I had to do was show some ID, and everything was gravy.

"Question, do you know Saya?" I asked the clerk.

"Of course, I work for your mother, Josephine Quinton."

"Cool, thanks."

I went up to the hotel suite, and got damn was this shit nice. I'd never been in a hotel this fresh in my damn life. I'd stayed in some nice ass places, traveling with my brothers and all, but this shit right here was otherworldly. I felt like I was in my damn condo almost. I would love to go on vacation or some shit with Summer and my baby girl, and stay in something like this, but I knew that shit was very unlikely.

After looking around, just admiring the suite, I scoped the scene so I could know where to hide, and where to escape if I needed to. I looked around the room, and checked for all the cameras to see if there in fact were any, and what they showed exactly. Once I was done, I got a text on my dummy phone from Saya, letting me know that the girl was on her way up with dude.

I slipped into the closet and made sure the shutters were adjusted to where I could see. While waiting inside, I twisted the silencer onto my gun, and then waited patiently.

About ten minutes later, I heard them enter the room. He was talking to her about some shit, and from her mannerisms, she wasn't too interested in what he had to say.

"I've ordered a bottle to be sent up for us already. I told Mrs. Wilbur when she booked the room to have the most expensive bottle sent up. Even though the cost of this suite was a pretty penny, I didn't mind spending the extra cash on you," he grinned, using my mother's fake name.

He reminded me of the actor Keith David, and I knew he was about fifty something years old. Ole girl looked no older than twenty-three, and had no business entertaining a nigga old enough to be her daddy. This was the business I guess.

"How much?" she questioned nervously as he ran his fingers up and down her small arm. Shorty was pretty as fuck, with vibrant caramel skin and shoulder length brown hair. Her body looked nice from what I could see under the sexy black dress.

"Almost ten grand, but I knew you would make it worth my while."

They began kissing and I cringed at the sight. I felt bad for shorty. I waited as they kissed some more, before he began removing her dress. Her titties sat up perfectly, and the sight of her brown nipples made my mouth water. He immediately began unbuckling himself, before placing her on all fours.

"Let me get a condom," she said.

"All the money I paid? I don't think so, sweetie. Plus, Mrs. Wilbur told me you were on birth control; that was what I requested," he growled and kissed her shoulders.

Using condoms was a part of my mom's policy, so that was never up for discussion. However, some of the girls weren't on the pill, so my mom gave clients the option to choose a girl who *was* on it, for an additional fee of course.

"Please, Mr. Atkins, I would prefer if you—" He cut her off by forcing a kiss on her mouth. "Mr. Atkins—"

"Shut the fuck up and hold still!" he barked.

I pushed open the closet just enough to fit the tip of my gun through, and once I had it aimed where I wanted, I fired.

PHEW!

"Ah! Fuck!" he shouted and grabbed his abdomen. I gagged when I saw his dick sticking out of his slacks.

Coming out of the closet, I made eye contact with the girl, before moving closer to the thirsty ass john.

"Who the fuck are you? Is this some kind of setup? Get me a medic!" he hollered as he stared up me, holding his side.

PHEW!

I said nothing before sending another bullet through his head.

"Fix yourself and meet me downstairs so I can take you home," I stated sternly before leaving out of the escape way that I'd found. I texted Saya that I had to kill him from my dummy phone, and she let me know the clean up crew was already at the hotel so she would let them know.

Speeding around to the front, I reached across the passenger seat, and pushed the door open so the girl could get in. She looked afraid still, and I felt a bit bad for her.

"You good?" I quizzed as we sped down Boylston.

"Ye-yes I'm fine." After a few moments of silence, she said, "Thank you, Rhys. I appreciate you coming out such last minute."

"No problem, shorty. You hungry?"

"No, he just took me to eat, but thank you again for helping me,

I really appreciate it. You can let me out here, I'm gonna get a room."

"You don't want to go home?"

"I don't have a home. I live in a hotel, if you will."

"What's your name?" I asked once I pulled over in front of the hotel.

"Indiya."

"Did he pay you?"

"Well, your mother got me the money before the date so I'm good."

"Aight then, be safe, shorty."

"I will." I watched until she entered the hotel, and then went home to shower, watch some TV, eat, and get high.

Just a normal day in the life of a Quinton.

I would be leaving town to go to Pittsburgh tomorrow night, so I had to make a few arrangements, namely making sure a bulletproof car would be there waiting for me. I never traveled in a non bulletproof car, and neither did anyone I cared about. My shorty's car was bulletproof as well. The higher up in shit you were, the more niggas hated you and wanted your spot. And in order to have your spot, they would need to get rid of you. That's with any business though, not just illegal shit.

Since I was coming right back out, I decided to just park out on the street by my condo instead of parking in the structure attached. When I pulled up, I saw Hayden standing outside with her back facing the street. I don't know why her ass insisted on coming over here, and then on top of that, she liked to wait outside like an idiot. Thankfully it was about 11am, so it wasn't as dangerous.

Jogging across the street, I made it onto the curb and walked right up to her annoying ass. Ever since she displayed that pitiful behavior at her job, I was completely turned off. Not like I had plans to be with her or anything, but I still found her sexy and attractive. Now, she was hella unappealing.

"Why are you showing up at my shit unannounced?" I asked,

irritated. "What if my shorty was here? If she saw you, we would have problems."

"Is that all you care about?" she turned to face me and I almost threw up. Her whole face was beat the fuck up, and she was crying.

"Shorty, what the fuck happened to you?"

"He-he found out," she cried.

"Calm down, ma. When did he do this?" I moved closer to get a better look. I despised niggas who hit females, it didn't matter how I felt about them.

"Like two weeks ago, and he killed Ingrid!" she hollered before pushing herself into my chest and sobbing.

"What? What the fuck is wrong with that nigga?" I frowned. I said it aloud, but I wasn't really expecting her to answer. How did Ingrid get into the mix? "Come up." I took her hand into mine, and led her up to my condo. "You want some water? Juice?" I asked once she sat down on my couch.

"No, I'm okay. I hate him," she wept.

"Aye, don't cry. I'm sorry about Ingrid; I know that was your best friend. But look, shorty, I'm gonna get that nigga for doing this shit to your face." I knelt down in front of her.

I was pissed as fuck that this nigga had done all this to her, and killed ole girl. I understood that he was upset that his bitch was getting fucked, but that was no reason to beat her ass like she was a nigga. She barely even looked the same, and I knew she needed medical attention. If he had have kept going, she would have most likely died.

"You are?" she looked down at me.

"Yeah, I am. I ain't gon' let that nigga get away with doing this shit to you. But baby girl, I need to get you to a hospital. You haven't been, have you?"

"No, you think it's that bad?"

"Yeah, I know it is. Get up so we can get you to a doctor. You hungry?"

"Yes, I've been craving Taco Bell," she giggled and stood up.

"Aight, I will take you by there."

I was about to turn away but she hugged me tightly. I hesitated, but then just hugged her back since I felt sorry for her.

"I love you, Tarenz. He beat me up because I told him I loved you, and it's true. I love you so much and I can't live without you." She tilted her head back to look up into my eyes.

"Hayden, shorty, don't do this right now, aight? I have love *for* you, but that's it. We discussed this, and I don't wanna talk about the shit anymore. I love you as a friend and nothing more, okay?"

She declined to respond, and just grabbed her purse from the couch. Walking to the door, she began weeping lightly again.

"You can just take me home; I will go to the hospital later."

"No, you will go now. Come on." I walked out of my door past her, then pulled her right along with me.

***

11pm that night...

I was inside Peel's condo, looking around at all of his shit. Like my brothers and I, his condo from the outside looked regular, but the inside was furnished with nothing but the best. I saw some stuff belonging to a female, and I guess they were Hayden's things.

After scoping his whole place, I took a spot behind the wall that was located next to an archway, leading to his bedrooms. I wanted this to be quick and easy. I was gonna fire an injury only shot, then a fatal one. That was how I always did shit, and that's the way I was taught by my father.

My phone chimed as I waited, and I looked down at it to see it was from Kimberlyn.

My Shorty: *Where are you?*

Me: *Be home soon.*

She texted me back, but I didn't feel like talking right now; I needed to stay focused.

Finally, I heard keys jingling in the door, and once Peel entered and closed it behind himself, I sent a bullet through his hip.

"Ah!" he yelled, collapsing to the ground in agony. "Who the fuck is here!" he shouted as he patted for his own gun.

PHEW!

I sent a silent shot into his hand, causing him to cry out again in pain. Finally revealing myself, we made eye contact, and the terror in his eyes was remarkable. I'd never seen a nigga so scared in my life.

"You bitch ass nigga," he groaned as I neared him.

"Hayden didn't think so."

"Fuck you!" he shouted, damn near through tears. "You're gonna lose that little bitch of yours, and I can't wait until it happens!" he coughed. "Gang and I should've ran a train on her," he grinned with blood on his lips.

PHEW!

I sent another shot into his shoulder, wanting him to suffer. By now he was crying like a little child, and blood was everywhere. Although I had on plastic shoe covers, I still didn't want his blood on my feet.

"TQ—"

PHEW!

I placed my gun under his chin, and blew his brains out. Brain matter was covering the bottom of his door, and the carpet area next to it. I left his crib discreetly, the same way that I'd snuck in, and then went to the warehouse to change and burn my clothes. I sprayed myself with a water hose because some of his brain got on my neck. After that, I was good to go.

When I got home, I immediately hopped into the shower, and once I was clean I went ahead and brushed my teeth. Coming out of the bathroom, I stopped in my tracks when I saw an angry Kimberlyn looking up into my face with tears in her eyes.

"What you doing? Move back so I can get out of the bathroom."

"How dare you cheat on me when I'm carrying your baby," she

grimaced and twisted her little face as if it were intimidating.

"What? What are you talking about, Kimberlyn? Move." I walked out of the bathroom past her, and then put some boxers on while she watched.

"This!" she shoved her phone in my face, and it was Hayden and I, holding hands and going into my condo. Fuck! *Who the fuck snapped those?* I wondered. Never mind I was sure it was someone from Gang's crew.

"Kimberlyn, relax, baby," I stated as she shook her head 'no' repeatedly.

"I'm leaving."

"So here we go again with you assuming shit and not letting me explain. If you leave this time, Kimberlyn, it's over for good. Now either you can let me explain the picture to you, or you can leave like some little child." She just stared at me, so I moved closer and tried to peck her but she stopped me. "Gang's homie Peel whooped her ass, and I was just bringing her inside so she could sit down and calm herself, Kimberlyn. I swear that was it."

"So where were you tonight?"

"I was handling some business and it didn't involve me fucking around on you, okay? Please don't start being one of those girls."

"One of what girls?" she raised her brow and folded her arms. I immediately regretted saying that statement.

"Nothing."

"No, tell me, Tarenz."

"One of those nagging ass bitches who be on their nigga's heads even though he ain't doing shit. You may need to stop kicking it with Summer, she's rubbing off on you."

"Fuck you," she said in a low tone before walking off.

I threw my head back and sighed before following after her. I was slightly thrown off track when I saw her notebook and laptop sprawled across my bed. This was not gonna work. After getting my mind back on the subject at hand, I hugged her from behind and kissed her neck.

"Stop letting all this shit get to you. You said yourself that people will always wanna break us up, right?" I asked and she nodded. "Exactly, so don't allow these niggas to break up our happy home. You got my baby and my heart, which means no woman could ever take your place." I kissed the corner of her mouth and witnessed her smile a little.

"I don't want you trying to make Hayden feel better, because if you can do that, then I can hang out with Gang."

"I guess that's fair." I let her go and she turned around to cup my face and kiss my lips. "Shorty, get all this shit off my bed, I'm ready to lie down."

"Oh, sorry," she giggled. "I told you I should be at my grandmother's more." She cleared the bed.

"No, just do your work in the living room until we figure something out."

Once she got everything off, I threw her on all fours, and pulled her shirt over her head. I then yanked down her panties, and she lifted her body a little so I could get them off. Quickly climbing off the bed,

I removed my boxers and then got back behind her. As soon as I got inside, chills dripped down my spine because of how good it felt.

"Baby, I want you to move back and forth on my dick," I instructed.

"Mmm," she tucked her lips in out of pleasure as her pussy throbbed around my dick. "You mean like, throw it back?"

"Yeah, fuck you know about that? But that's exactly what I mean, just slowly."

She nodded and then began to move back and forth on my dick. The sight was more than a nigga could have ever dreamed of. I found myself moaning lowly just from looking.

"Spread your legs more."

She did as I asked and continued gliding up and down my dick, coating it with her nectar. This woman's pussy was the fucking truth, and no one could blame me for shooting up the club and getting her pregnant. She could run the world with this shit she had between her legs. It was always so wet, warm, and snug, pulling me in with every stroke.

"Uuuh," she trembled as she released. So sexy.

I gripped her shoulder to stop her movements, and then made her lay flat. I spread her legs some, and then entered her while she laid on her stomach. Wrapping her long hair around my hand, I began pulverizing her shit, causing us both to holler loudly.

"Baby, fuck," I grunted and frowned.

"Mmm, uuhhh, Tarenz," she whimpered as I plowed into her ferociously from the back.

I sped up even more, and before I knew it, I was cumming all inside of her. We both began to breathe heavily, and once I caught my breath, I rolled off of her. I lied on my back, and then tugged her on top of me so she could lay on my chest.

"Sorry about earlier," she whispered as she stared down into my face.

"You're good. If you *weren't* jealous I should be worried, I guess."

"I see we both make one another jealous. That means we really love each other, huh?"

"I guess so, shorty."

She slipped her tongue into my mouth, and we tongued it up until we were ready to go another round.

Goldie

Britain and I had finally landed in New York, New York about an hour ago. We were just now getting into our suite at the Conrad New York, a beautiful hotel in Lower Manhattan. Our suite was huge, and I'm sure it cost Britain a nice amount of money. I knew he only endured the best all the time, but a part of me would like to think that he was doing a little bit to impress me.

"This is a nice ass suite. Would you have stayed here if I wasn't with you?" I smirked.

"Maybe, but you being here was a big part of the decision," he smiled, making me smile as well.

"Where does your woman think you are?"

"I told you she's not my woman anymore, and is this really the time to ask that? You should've asked before we boarded the jet."

"Whoa, relax, I just wanted to know. It doesn't make a difference to me, I'm just accompanying a friend on a trip, nothing more."

He laughed and asked, "So you're not here because you like me and miss me tearing that little pussy to shreds?"

"Nope, not at all," I replied before we both burst into laughter.

"Well, I will be the mature one and admit that I missed you and

I wanted you to come with me because I didn't want to wait until I got back to see you."

I was a bit in disbelief at what was coming out of this man's mouth. We went from agreeing to be just fuck buddies to him missing me. I missed him too, but I just wasn't expecting him to feel the same way. Yeah, he bugged me constantly since I beat Tekeya's ass, but I just thought he wanted to fuck.

"I missed you too." I plopped down on the couch. He sat next to me, and then pulled me into his lap.

"So what's up? We gon' do this?"

"Do what?" I frowned.

"Be a couple, shorty."

"Who said I wanted to be with you, Britain? I don't even know if you're really broken up with your girlfriend or not, and I'll be damned if I'm oblivious to your acts."

"I told you I'm not with her. We hashed everything out, and agreed to go our separate ways."

This nigga must've thought I was a damn fool. That girl was crazy, no, psycho about him, and I highly doubt she would let him go that easily. She had her claws deeply dug into him, and it would take more than a conversation and a park fight to remove them.

"Britain, please. If you did talk to her, I am sure it went left."

"Okay, you got me. She took off on me, and then her home girl called the police, who then caught me with my hand around her neck."

"Oh shit," I chuckled. "So she knocked you out and called the police? At least they didn't put you in jail."

"Only because one of the officers is on my dad's payroll. They had me in cuffs and everything, ready to take my ass downtown until he showed up."

"Dang, she really is crazy. But can you blame her? She loves you and now you're acting funny," I caressed the side of his face.

"But she knows I'm not happy, and I don't even see how she's been happy. We barely talk, unless we're fighting, and we barely fuck. I was fucking the hoes more than her, that was until you came along."

"And what happened when I came along?"

"You got me hooked on that good, and I was only craving it." He kissed my neck and groped my thigh.

"You make me feel bad."

"Huh?"

"No," I giggled. "The sex is bomb, but I'm saying I feel bad for breaking up your relationship."

"You didn't break up anything, baby. I was halfway out of the door when I met you. You just gave me the courage to make a decision that I should've made almost a year ago."

"Really?" I played with his dreads. He was so damn sexy. His lips were so full that I just had to kiss them.

"Yeah, really. Why you stop?" he questioned, referring to the kiss.

"Didn't you say you were gonna take me to dinner?"

"Oh yeah, let's get ready then," he sighed as I got up. "You are way too sexy for words, yo." He ran his hands over his face as I sauntered away. The bulge in his pants told me dinner wasn't even on his mind.

***

I was now showered, smelling good, and looking sexy. My makeup was flawless, and gave off a natural look. My mustard colored dress was tight and short, and my heels were high, accentuating my already sexy legs. I let my golden brown locks hang down since unbeknownst to Britain, I'd gotten my hair done for the trip.

"Damn, shorty, I didn't even know you could look any better than you already did." He peeked into the bathroom as I looked myself over.

He was wearing all black, and it gave him a mysterious look. His dreads were hanging loosely, sweeping his broad shoulders, which were covered by a black button up. His jeans were really dark, and so were his Adidas. He was iced out, but not too much to where he looked like an unintelligent rapper. All in all, the nigga looked good and the smell of his cologne was on that same level.

"I love your cologne," I had to admit as I walked out of the bathroom. "What is it?" I asked as if I didn't know.

"Jo Malone London," he replied. "And thanks. You ready?"

"Yes."

He opened the hotel room door for me, and then I walked out. Once he joined me in the hallway, we held hands and headed down to a restaurant named Atrio, located in the hotel. Britain said it was a really good upscale restaurant with a nice view, and since I'd never been to New York, I didn't argue it.

"I have a reservation for Britain Quinton," he told the hostess once we got there.

I smiled because sadly, I'd never been on a date where the person needed to make reservations. Ethan was my first and last boyfriend, and he just wasn't that type of nigga. Britain was an elegant thug, where as Ethan was just a thug through and through, no special additions. I preferred Britain's type any day though.

Once we were seated, our drink orders were taken, and we were given a few moments to look over the menu. Every dish had a nice price tag next to it, but Britain assured me that it was beyond fine for me to get what I wanted.

After looking for about ten minutes, he asked, "What would you like so I can order it for you?"

"What do you mean? Why can't I just tell the waiter?" I smiled.

"I guess you can do that. I was just raised that way. My father always ordered for himself and my mother," he shrugged. He was so cute.

"Okay, I guess it's fine. I want the Hanger Steak, medium."

"Good choice. I hate when people get well done. As my father says, you cook all the damn flavor out," he grinned and so did I, as I admired his beautiful blue eyes.

"Here are your drinks." The waiter set them down. "Are you two ready to order?"

"Yes, my girlfriend and I will both have the Hanger Steak, cooked medium, please," Britain responded. Hearing him call me his girlfriend made me feel all warm and fuzzy inside.

"Great choice. And are the caramelized onions okay on both?"

"Yes," he nodded after looking to me to get the okay.

"Girlfriend?" I raised a brow once the waiter skated away.

"Yeah, I told you I wanted you to be my girlfriend. I know yo' ass said no, but I didn't know what else to call you just now."

"I see. I mean, I don't mind being your girlfriend, I'm just a little scared, you know?" I looked into his eyes before glancing out the window to see the beautiful night view of the lower Manhattan skyline. He was right; the view was exceptional.

"Scared of what?"

"Well, multiple things. I'm afraid that being with you will bring me a lot of unnecessary drama. Also, you don't have the greatest track record, and I'm not trying to bounce from one cheater to another. But most importantly, I'm scared that someone will be able to steal you away like I did from Tekeya."

"Shorty, you didn't steal me away. A man cannot be stolen, no person can be stolen if they didn't already want to leave. When I met you, Tekeya and I were not happy, I told you that."

"What went wrong?" I sipped my drink.

"She's too insecure, and I don't like anyone putting their hands on me, female or not. And the fact that I can't hit her ass back irks me sometimes."

"I mean didn't she have reason to be insecure? It's not like you were being this wonderful faithful boyfriend."

"True. I mean, I did some dirt here and there, I will admit. But she took me back, and if she knew she couldn't get over it, she should have let me go."

"I agree, that's why I had to break it off with Ethan. Did you ever love her? Do you love her now?" Please say no, I thought.

"I never loved Tekeya. There was a point where I really did care for her, and I thought we would get there, but no, I never loved her. I got with her for the wrong reasons. She was fine as fuck, and all the niggas wanted her, so I got with her as like an ego thing. She was never someone I felt I was gonna marry, and our shit just lasted longer than I had intended because I didn't care to break it off. But now, I've realized that it was long overdue."

"Well now that I know more, I don't mind being your girlfriend. Are you sure you want me as a girlfriend? I mean, you just came from a relationship."

"That wasn't a relationship, that was a burden. And yes, I'm very ready for you to be my girl. You know I ain't never talked on the phone or got on FaceTime with a girl until you?"

"Wait, never?"

"Well, I've talked on the phone, mainly in high school and in my late teens, but it was just mundane conversations that I held because I wanted to fuck. With you, we have real conversations and I haven't done that. Tekeya and I only texted a lot."

"I feel special then," I cheesed.

"You should."

"I won't be your girlfriend just yet though. We should spend more time together so you can see if you really want this."

"How do I know if you really want me as a boyfriend?" he bit his plump bottom lip.

"Oh, I do. And I have for much longer than I've known you."

"True, because every time I saw you, your ass was staring a damn hole through me, shorty."

"Whatever," I chuckled, trying to change the subject since I was embarrassed.

The food didn't take too long to come, and after eating it and dessert, we retired to the suite. We were gonna walk around, but we were both beat from flying and shit. We hadn't laid down once.

"Thank you for dinner, goodnight." I stood on my tiptoes to kiss his cheek, and then headed to the bathroom. I chuckled because I could feel him watching me.

Stripping down, I climbed into the shower and let the hot water run all over my body. I was gonna sleep good tonight after this bomb ass shower. I closed my eyes to think for a little bit, when I felt a presence behind me. I slowly turned around, and there stood Britain in all his nakedness.

"Britain—"

"Shut up." He lifted me up, and brought me down on his dick before I could say anything.

Pain and pleasure shot through my body as his dick invaded it repeatedly. I hadn't been touched since we had that little session in the car at the park, and that only lasted a couple minutes.

He was holding me up as if I were equal to a feather, while gliding me up and down his shaft. We kissed hungrily, moaning into one another's mouths in the process. It felt so good and right for some reason, even though to others I'm sure it was wrong. Spreading my legs wider, he sped up his pumps, prompting me to holler out as if I were Patti LaBelle. I came after only ten seconds.

"Shit," he grumbled, before sucking my lips into his mouth. "This pussy, man."

Our skin was smacking together loudly as he drilled me roughly yet passionately. My body stiffened, and then released everything I had inside of me. Britain wasn't too far behind.

We kissed for a few moments, and then he let me down so we could wash off. We then got into the same bed, and he cuddled behind me. After kissing my shoulder and the nape of my neck, he tightened his grip on my body before we drifted off to sleep.

CHAPTER FOUR

Lendsey

One week later...

Matikah had me going fucking crazy, and I didn't like it at all. I was Lendsey Quinton, I didn't have to chase any woman, but oddly, Matikah had me acting like some thirsty ass nigga who couldn't take a hint. I didn't care how many times she told me she didn't want me, I wasn't stopping until she changed her answer. I was in love, and as much as it made me cringe, it was true.

Hitting ignore on Dania who had called me for the twentieth time today, I climbed out of my car and walked around onto the sidewalk. I jogged up Matikah's grandmother's porch steps, and hit the doorbell immediately. I was damn near sweating, waiting for her to answer the door. I couldn't wait to see that pretty innocent face, even though I'm sure it would be knotted up in a frown.

"Lendsey?" her grandmother opened the door.

"Oh hi, Mrs. Hudson, I—"

"Call me Luna. Matikah isn't here at the moment, Lendsey."

"Where the hell- excuse me, where is she?"

"Relax," she chuckled. "She's off taking her cosmetology final right now. She will be home in about twenty minutes if you'd like to wait." She opened the screen, and stood to the side so that I could come in.

"Actually, this works out because I'd like to talk to you about Matikah." I closed the door behind me.

"Oh?" she sat down on the couch, and moved some sales magazines out the way so that I could join her.

"I need you to tell me what to do to convince her to give me another chance. I've tried everything, I'm not sure if she's told you, but I have. If you could just tell me what would make her come back, I would be forever grateful for you. I have my checkbook." She chuckled at my last statement.

"Well, before I do that, I need to know if you've really changed. I don't want Matikah to be with you if you're just going to continue to break her heart like you've done."

"I swear I wouldn't be doing all of this if I wasn't planning on changing my ways Mrs.- Luna. I love her, I really do, and I just had a moment of weakness that I will never have again."

"You sure?" she raised her brow, and gestured towards my phone in my hand. It was on silent, but the screen was lit up, displaying Dania's name. Shit, Dania and I finally had something in common; we were thirsty for people who didn't want our asses.

"Sorry about that." I hit ignore. "But yes, I'm very sure. Only thing that matters to me right now is being with Matikah."

"I can see the desperation in your eyes, and I can tell that you're in love with my grand baby, so I will give you a bit of advice. Just tell her how you feel."

"That's it?" I frowned. I thought she was gonna give me something else, something better.

"Yes, that's it. Tell her how you feel, and how much it hurts being apart from her. Look her in the eyes and let her see what I'm seeing right now. She doesn't just want to hear how much you miss her, she wants to know why."

"Okay, okay," I nodded, taking it all in. "I will do that, thank you—"

"What is he doing here?" Matikah walked in the door, looking beautiful as ever. She had on tights and a white t-shirt, but because I was pining for her so, she looked like she was dressed for the red carpet. Damn, this girl had me sick as fuck.

"Matikah, let me—"

"No, you need to leave. You're doing too much, and it's not very becoming of you, Lendsey."

"Matikah, let the boy talk, damn," her grandmother chimed in, and I was thanking God for her right now.

"Really, Ma?"

"Yes, really." She raised her brow at Matikah, who blew out hot air and rolled her eyes. I laughed at her mean ass.

"I will leave you two." Her grandmother got up to grab her jacket and keys. "I have to go to the grocery store."

"Come with me to my condo so I can talk to you."

"No, we talk here or I'm not talking to you at all." She walked to her bedroom and I followed behind her.

She sat down on her bed, and I knelt down in front of her to take her hands into mine. Looking up into her face, I admired how pretty she was. I could tell I still made her a bit nervous, because she would look away uncomfortably every now and then.

"Matikah, baby, I want to apologize not only for stepping out on you, but for trying to justify the fact that I did. I just want you to know that this time apart from you really had me thinking, and I've realized that life is much better *with* you. I've been for real sick, ma. like I can barely sleep through the night because I can't get you off my mind. I hardly have an appetite, and I can't even focus at work because of you. I feel like I'm going insane. I love you, shorty, and I swear if you give me a chance I will always be good to you and make you happy," I kissed her hands.

She snatched them to wipe the tear that was traveling down her face, and then looked back into my eyes for a couple moments. She said nothing, but then she burst into tears; not the reaction I was expecting.

"Matikah, what are you crying for?" I picked her face up from her hands and kissed her lips a couple times. Thumbing her tears away, I leaned in to kiss her again as she sniffled. "You love me?" I whispered and she nodded. "Can we be back together?" She nodded and a nigga almost wanted to get up and tap dance like Gregory Hines.

I immediately dipped my tongue into her mouth, while pulling her tights and panties down. I needed some, and not just from anybody, but from her specifically. I tossed her bottoms to the side, and then pulled away to take off her shirt and bra. She watched me as I undressed, and then I climbed between her legs to kiss her. Our bodies were pressed so closely together you would think we were trying to become one. Kissing her passionately, I pushed myself into her, watching her face twist up as she sniveled.

"I love you, baby," I whispered, as I moved in and out of her lethal ass box. "Don't ever leave me again."

"I won't." She quivered from cumming.

A nigga finally had his shorty back…

Summer

Hakim: Will be there in about an hour.

Tonight I had a date with Hakim. I was beyond excited to have a redo, and have it not end with Rhys beating him to a bloody pulp. I still couldn't believe his ass did that, but that was my crazy ass baby daddy for you. The only thing Rhys brought with him was violence.

Hakim was so different from Rhys, and if this did progress, I'm sure it would be much less stressful than being with Rhys, which excited me on its own. I was still in love with my ex, but it was slowly dwindling, and I couldn't wait for my feelings to be completely gone. I grinned in the mirror just from thinking about it. I'd prayed for the longest to be able to get over Rhys, and I think God was finally listening.

"You look pretty, Mommy!" Bryleigh stood in my doorway.

She'd given her Barbie a haircut, and the shit was fly. I guess I knew what she would be when she grew up, because if she could cut bobs like that at four years old, there's no telling what she could do twenty years from now.

"I do? Thank you," I smiled at her as she nodded with her eyes closed.

Hakim and I were only going to the movies, so I chose to wear a t-shirt dress with sneakers. I let my dreads hang down my back, and only wore a watch and necklace. I wanted to be cute but not too dressed up since it was just the movies.

Seeing Bryleigh made me wonder where her father was. He was coming to get her tonight and keeping her for the weekend, but he still wasn't here. *He better not flake.* Grabbing my phone, I went to text him but I heard a knock at the door.

"Bry, do not open the door!" I yelled when she darted out of the bedroom. She'd made a habit out of answering the door before even knowing who it was. I think it was because she could finally reach the doorknob.

"Daddy!" I heard her squeal.

"Bryleigh, I told you not to open the door until I got there!" I spat as I walked into the living room to see Rhys holding her.

He looked so good, even though he wasn't dressed up at all. He just had on a hoodie, basketball shorts, socks, and some Nike slides. I could smell his Versace cologne though, and I kind of missed it. Rhys' outside was perfect, it was just his tormented insides.

"I'm sorry, Mommy, but I knew who it was already!" She giggled and hugged her father's neck tightly. I knew she missed him just as much as I did.

"Listen to your mother, okay Bry?" Rhys looked into her eyes.

"Okay."

"Where you headed?" he asked as his eyes scanned me from head to toe.

"I told you I was going out, Rhys."

"With some friends or what?" he frowned, and both he and Bryleigh stared at me waiting for an answer.

"Why would you ask that in front of her? But if you must know, I'm going on a date." I turned on my heels and then went to my bedroom to grab my purse and phone. Thank God Hakim had texted me that he'd arrived. I made sure to text and tell him to stay downstairs, because I did not feel like witnessing another beat down, and I'm sure he had no interest in receiving another. "You're still here?" I asked when I walked into the living room.

"Calm the fuck down, aight? Don't be talking to me like I fucking disgust you or some shit. Bryleigh forgot something in her room and I'm waiting for her, is that cool?" he hissed.

"Just lock up when you leave." I rushed out because although most times I hated when he got angry, he'd just turned me on.

Walking down and out of my building, I spotted Hakim's Mercedes and headed over. He didn't get out to open the door for me, but I guess it was no big deal. I was used to Rhys getting out of the car to do so, but I had to remind myself that there were way worse attributes that Rhys had and Hakim didn't.

"Hello, beautiful," Hakim smiled. His face had completely healed by now, but there were still a few imperfections. At work, Paul let him do a few ab shots but nothing facial yet. I prayed that his face returned to normal completely, because if not, I would forever feel like I was to blame.

"Hey, you smell good."

"So do you." He leaned over and kissed my cheek before speeding down my street.

***

"How did you like the movie?"

"I really loved it. I honestly think it was better than *Finding Nemo*, don't you?" I looked over at him as I buckled my seat belt. We'd just come from seeing *Finding Dory.*

"I agree. I didn't think it would be able to top it but it did. I can't believe I'm a grown ass man seeing these kinds of movies."

"It's cool. I like that about you."

"Oh, ya boy never took you to see kid's movies?" he asked as he backed out of the parking space.

"Yeah, he has because we have a daughter together, but he would be annoyed if it was just he and I going."

"I'm not like that. I aim to please, especially when it comes to my woman, so I would never complain about something that you wanted to do."

"I can tell, and it's refreshing," I smiled, more so to myself.

After driving for a while, we made it to Neptune Oyster on Salem. It was a pretty pricey seafood restaurant that I'd gone to before with Rhys. I was happy to know Hakim had good taste, and enjoyed fine dining every now and then. I couldn't go from expensive dining to burger joints; my ex had me spoiled.

Getting out of the car, he again reached for my hand to hold it. Funny enough, we both looked over our shoulders at the same time because of what happened the last time we decided to embrace. We burst into laughter when we realized what we'd done. I kind of liked that he could laugh about it. It just showed me how much more laid back he was over Rhys.

"I really am sorry about how our last date ended."

"I told you that you don't have to keep apologizing, Summer. Don't be sorry for that nigga's mistakes, okay?" I just nodded.

Once we were seated, we ordered drinks and looked over the menu for a bit. After placing our food order, we were left to ourselves to chat a bit. I will admit that this was weird for me because I hadn't been on a date with a man who wasn't Rhys since… well, it just never happened. That's if you don't count that horrifying night with Rhys kicking Hakim's ass.

"So Hakim, why are you single? I mean, I'm sure you've had plenty of prospects with being a model and all."

"Yeah I have, but I'm not into women who throw themselves at me. I like the chase. I mean, I don't like women who play games, but I don't want to get it that easily because that means I'm not the only one who can."

"Makes sense."

"So you and your child's father are done for good?"

"Absolutely. I've been with him for a very long time, and it doesn't seem like he will ever grow up. I want to get married and stuff, and I also want to be able to have adult conversations without feeling like I'm gonna have to box in a minute." I swallowed hard after I spoke, because I was still uncomfortable with badmouthing Rhys to another man.

I didn't care to remind Hakim of the fact that a bitch Rhys cheated on me with shot me. It was embarrassing to even think about. Sometimes I wish that Hakim wasn't the one who had taken me to the hospital, because I didn't want him to know about it.

"Totally understandable. Hopefully a new woman he meets will make him better," he sighed, as the waitress set down our cocktails.

Hearing him say that angered me, because that would break my heart if another woman were able to make Rhys faithful and calm. I knew my mom said I would have to accept it, but I wasn't ready to face that truth.

"I doubt it," I chuckled and sipped my drink.

"Doubt what?"

"I doubt that a new woman will be able to make him become a better man."

"Don't, because that's how it works. I'm telling you as a man, if we really want someone, we will change like that," he snapped his fingers. "It doesn't take us years and years to change. The only time that happens is when we're holding onto you until we find something better."

"Rhys loves me."

"Maybe he does but—"

"No, it's not a maybe, he does."

"Hey Summer, I didn't mean to offend you. I'm just simply trying to give you some advice, and an insight on how us men think. We don't stay set in our ways if we really love a woman and she wants us to change."

"Let's talk about something else because I can feel this conversation going the wrong way."

"Are you sure you're over him? You seem pretty upset, baby."

"I am over him; I just don't like that you're insinuating that he doesn't love me because I know he does."

"If you were over him, it wouldn't matter."

"Take me home." I placed the cloth napkin on the table and scooted out of the booth we were sitting in. He was irritating me, and in a minute, I was gonna repeat what Rhys did to his ass.

"Summer, wait baby, relax. We can talk about something else. I don't want to talk about your ex anyway." He grabbed my wrist when I tried to walk by him. "Please sit."

I stared down at him angrily, before finally sitting down again. I was ready to go, but the only thing stopping me was the fact that I really wanted that North End Cioppino dish I'd ordered. I sipped my drink and kept going until there was none left, before waving the waitress over to get me another. For the rest of the dinner, we only made small talk as I scarfed down my food and tossed back cocktail after cocktail on his dime.

***

"Are you gonna be upset at me forever?" he asked and rubbed my thigh, since we'd been riding in the car in silence. I smacked his hand away, making him chuckle. "I am sorry, Summer. I admit I was a bit out of bounds for trying to tell you how your ex felt about you when I don't even know the gist of the situation."

"Very out of bounds."

"Do you accept my apology?"

"Yes, I guess."

"Thank you. Did you want to come to my house for coffee? We didn't get to do that last time."

"No, I need to go home. I have work very early tomorrow since I agreed to help Paul with tomorrow's models."

"Understandable. When can I see you again, if I can?"

"I'm off Thursday, so we can go out Wednesday night."

"Sounds good." He turned onto Confidential where my condo was located, and pulled over. "Tonight was nice, even though we hit a bump in the road."

"Yeah, it was. See you later." I kissed his cheek, got out, and then power walked into my building. "Really?" I walked into my condo to see Rhys sitting there sipping some dark liquor and watching TV.

"Really what?" he frowned.

"Why are you here? And where is Bry?"

"She's asleep, and I'm here because I wanted to make sure you came home tonight. Why else would I be here?"

"Why would you need to make sure I got home, Rhys?" I rolled my eyes and walked to check on Bryleigh, before going into my bedroom. He followed me the whole way.

"To make sure you didn't fuck him, and that he didn't try anything with you."

"We are not together anymore, so there is no need for you to keep tabs on my pussy, okay?" I took my earrings off.

He was quiet, and as I took my tennis shoes off he neared, towering over me like the Empire State Building. Once my shoes were off, he got all in my space and face, before pressing his lips against mine. Holding my jaw with his strong but gentle hands, he kissed me hungrily. I held onto his forearms as we made love with our mouths, and every part of this kiss told me that Hakim was wrong like I'd thought. Rhys loved me, he did.

"Rhys, move," I said in a low tone, pulling my lips from his.

"Summer, I did not cheat on you, shorty, I swear. Chenaye was just a friend and nothing more, I promise. She rolled up on me while I was waiting on the food I got you, and—"

"I really don't have the energy for this conversation. You need to go, and you can leave Bryleigh since she's sleep. Just get her tomorrow."

He stared at me in disbelief almost before saying, "Nah, umm, I know how to carry her without waking her." He looked into my eyes with his deep blue ones, before turning around and leaving the room.

I was still very much in love with Rhys Quinton, but I'm sure it would soon pass. Hopefully…

Kimberlyn

Saturday afternoon...

TQ's mother wanted to make lunch for us, so we were over there relaxing until the food was ready. She was making my favorite, barbecue wings, and I couldn't wait to tear into them. Being pregnant had me acting like a human garbage disposal. Every day I swore I would slow down on food, but it seemed like someone was always pushing a new meal in my face. My grandmother said it was better to feed the baby than starve it though, so that was my excuse to eat what I wanted.

"Son, can I talk to you?" TQ's father, Stony, walked into the den, wearing a distressed expression.

He gave me a weird smile, and I knew it was because he wasn't very fond of me. He must've really cherished his relationship with Gang, because TQ let me know that Gang complained to Stony about TQ and I being together, and in return his father asked him to drop me. I was just happy TQ wasn't some bitch nigga willing to give me up because his daddy said so. Honestly, I was waiting for his dad to show up and offer me money to leave him.

"Aight. Are you okay? You need anything before I go?" TQ looked at me.

"I'm fine, and stop acting like you're leaving or something," I smiled. He planted a kiss on my lips, and we got into it, forgetting his father was there until he cleared his throat.

Once TQ left, his mother brought me some chips and salsa to snack on while she cooked. As she was walking out, TQ's sister, Saya, entered with her boyfriend, Aries. She was wearing some shorts and a tube top like me, except her shorts were lighter, and her top was white. I had on dark distressed shorts, and my tube top was blue.

"I guess great minds think alike," she smiled and reached her arms out for a hug.

"I know!" I stood up to embrace her, before looking at her boyfriend and smiling.

Aries was a nice looking guy, and everything about him screamed thoroughbred thug. He even wore those corduroy slippers, and kept a wooden brush in his pocket to slide over his waves every now and then. Saya could do so much better in my opinion, as far as goal wise. I mean, she had a lot of money, her own money, and Aries didn't seem to be about shit. He seemed like the typical attractive guy who used females to get what he wanted because he could. I was sure that any money he had was given to him by Saya. He was handsome though, so I guess that was enough.

"You know my man, right?" she pointed to him.

"Yeah, I met him at your birthday party," I nodded and sat back down. I didn't want to be away from my chips and salsa too much longer.

"Oh yeah, I forgot about that. So I see you and my brother are still going strong. I haven't known him to have a girlfriend ever, so that says a lot." She sat next to me.

"Never?" I quizzed and glanced from her to Aries, who was not interested in whatever we were talking about. He was texting and smiling.

"Nope, never. You and your little friends have done a number on my little brothers, but in a good way. Do you guys have another friend hidden somewhere for Rhys?"

"No, we don't. Plus, Summer and I are friends so I couldn't exactly hook him up. It wouldn't feel right."

"I guess so. I love Summer but that girl is as insecure as they come, you know?"

"Umm, maybe," I shrugged. I didn't want to agree because I felt like I would be insulting my friend, and I didn't want to engage in that.

"You're loyal, I like that. Refusing to talk bad about a friend. Well, I hope you would do the same for me," she smiled.

"Of course, you're my future sister-in-law," I chuckled.

"Now if you get TQ to marry you, you will need to teach a class on how to tame a dog!" she joked, making us both laugh.

"My baby isn't a dog, he just needed the right amount of love that's all."

"I like that. You know—"

"Aye, Saya, get me something to drink," Aries cut her off rudely. "A beer, and not that Russian shit ya pops be buying."

"Okay, just—"

"Nah, now." He stared into her eyes, and I could see that he was talking to her through them. Whatever he was saying couldn't have been positive because she hopped up so quickly that I felt a wind. "So what's up with you?" he asked once she left.

"Huh?" I looked to him.

"I asked what was up with you?"

"Umm, what do you mean?" I honestly didn't know what the fuck he was referring to. Usually that question meant he was interested in me, but I wanted to give him the benefit of the doubt.

"I'm asking how you are, shorty." *Thank God.*

"Oh I'm fine. How are you?"

"I'm straight. How old are you?"

"I'm twenty-one, will be twenty-two in March of next year."

"Oh, okay, cool. So you're a Pisces or an Aries?" he smirked.

"Hey, my mom asked me to go to the store because she needs more cheese for the macaroni," Saya walked in, handing a topless beer to Aries.

"Oh alright, get me some hot chips please," he sipped it, staring up at her.

"You're not gonna come with me? I may need help."

"With cheese, ma?"

"No, I may have more stuff. She's making a list for me right now, Aries. Can you just come with me?"

"No, I don't want to. And if there is a lot of shit, I will help you unload when you get back." She stared down at him for a little bit, and then turned to face me.

"Would you like to come?"

"Saya, leave people alone and bounce!" he barked. She stormed out, and I didn't know whether to get up and go with her, or stay put. "Now what was I saying? Oh yeah, are you a Pisces or an Aries?"

"I'm an Aries, March twenty-sixth, and TQ is March twenty-eight, funny enough," I grinned at the thought.

"Didn't ask about him, but that's dope, shorty. You're an Aries and my name is Aries." *Point being?* I thought.

I was about to speak, but the sound of yelling coming from down the hallway caught me off guard. It sounded like TQ and his father, which I hoped that it wasn't. Suddenly, I saw his mother Josephine rush towards the ruckus. I stood up, and before I could, TQ was rushing into the den with his mother on his heels.

"Stop putting bullshit over business, fool!" his father yelled from down the hall, before slamming his office door. TQ started off back towards him, but his mother got in the way to stop him.

"Come on, baby, we will umm, I will take you to eat," he said and grabbed my jacket from the couch.

"Tarenz, baby, don't leave. I'm making this dinner for you guys," his mother pleaded.

"Sorry, Ma, I will come back another time, okay?" he kissed her cheek, and took my hand into his. I looked over my shoulder to see Aries wearing a smug expression. When he saw me looking, he put his two fingers up, and flicked his tongue between them, making me immediately look away.

"What happened?" I asked once we got into the car.

"Just know that me helping Hayden fucked some stuff up, but it's cool."

"Stuff like what?"

"Don't even concern you, shorty. Where do you want to eat?"

Saya Quinton

Two days later...

As I approached my condo door, I heard Drake's "Right Hand" blasting from inside my place. Rolling my eyes, I stuck the key in and entered. I was tired from dealing with the girls, appointments, and payroll all day, and didn't feel like entertaining Aries and his homies; especially not in my million-dollar condominium.

Before I got in the door good, I was slapped in the face with a cloud of smoke. Waving it from my vision, I continued in to see Aries smoking on my couch with his friend Jamie. I couldn't stand Jamie because he was a bad influence. My father always taught me that you are what you surround yourself with, and that was definitely true. Jamie wasn't about shit, and never would be about shit, so I hated for Aries to hang with his ass so much. He made Aries feel like not doing shit all day was cool, and it explained why Aries didn't do shit all day but smoke, eat, drive one of my Maseratis, and blow me up, asking for money while I was working.

People like Jamie was one of the reasons that I didn't have many female friends. Girls my age were on some other shit, and we just didn't get along. I didn't care about the shit that they did, because all

I loved was stacking my paper. I had one good home girl, Chloe, but even sometimes she was too annoying for me to be around. She didn't understand that in my life, getting my paper came first. Some nights I can't go to the club because I have to make sure my business is right. Plus, I'm Saya Quinton, so any venue I enter needs to be scoped out prior to my arrival, and have QCF security loaded.

"Party's over," I said before cutting on the huge oscillating fan in the living room, and turning down my sound system that Aries was about to break.

"Damn, hi to you too, Saya," Jamie smacked his lips. He didn't like me because he felt like I was a shady hoe. He didn't have to say it; I already knew it.

See, Jamie and Aries used to hang out with this dude named Pharaoh, who had the biggest crush on me. Pharaoh and I were just getting to know one another before he got locked up. When he did, Aries and I became close, and here we were together still, four years later. Jamie and Aries already had some animosity towards Pharaoh because my father gave him a job within the crime family, but not them. But even though Jamie didn't care too much for Pharaoh, he felt it was wrong for me to go from one friend to the other.

I do agree to an extent that it wasn't the best decision in the world for me to start dating Aries after Pharaoh got locked up, but to be honest, we were just cool. People knew Pharaoh liked me, but all we did was hang out a couple times. We'd never kissed, nor had we ever slept together, so I wasn't about to hold him down while he was in jail. Don't get me wrong, if he was my man I definitely would have been down for him, but he wasn't and that was all there was to it. At least he would be out in ten months though.

Ignoring Jamie's attitude, I went to my bedroom so I could put my purse down and take off these six-inch heels. My feet were barking like crazy, and I just wanted to take a hot bath, then soak them in my little pedicure tub. Turning my nose up at the smell of the weed, I quickly rushed back to the living room to reinforce the fact that the party was indeed over.

"Goodbye, Jamie," I folded my arms.

"Man, you gon' let her kick me out this shit?" he looked to Aries who was so high that I was sure he was floating a little.

"Let me? Nigga, this is my million-dollar condo that I pay the bills up in. If y'all want to get high all night and play video games, go to your baby mama's house, or to Aries' mother's!" I spat.

"Deuces, nigga," Jamie shot up off the couch. I was right on his heels, slamming the door behind him.

Before I could make it down the hall to get a towel for my bath, Aries had me hemmed up against the wall, with his big forearm pressed against my neck. He was applying a lot of pressure, and I knew if he pressed on my neck any harder I would die.

"Fuck did I tell you about embarrassing me and shit?!" He slammed me up against the wall before releasing the pressure off of my neck.

"Ho-how did I embarrass you?" I asked while panting heavily.

"Throwing around the fact that you pay all the bills up in this shit, Saya! Always running that fucking mouth for no damn reason! Then bringing up the fact that I live with my mama? Really?" He acted as if Jamie didn't know he lived with his damn mama.

"My bad, I forgot you lie to your friends to make them think you live and pay some bills here to help me." I really didn't know why he lied, because niggas knew my pockets were fat and that I in no way needed help from some thirty-three-year-old carless bum who lived with his mother. I was twenty-nine, fly, and balling.

Before I could finish my sarcastic apology, he'd gripped my jaw and began squeezing it. I hated when he did that shit because it hurt, and always left a bruise on my flawless dark skin.

"I'm not fucking around with you, shorty! Quit running your mouth before I fuck you up! You know I hit bitches! I ain't like these other niggas who think beating a woman's ass is a sin!"

"Okay!" A tear slid out of my eye due to the pain.

"Now, if you would talk to your dad or have one of your brothers let me work beside them, I wouldn't have to lie or live with my mama," he let my jaw go.

Moving it around, I closed my eyes to massage the sore parts. Some days I wondered why I was with this nigga, but I knew it was mainly due to his head game. His dick was cool, but the head would have you ready to put a bullet in any bitch who tried to sit on his face. I loved sex, and the thought of leaving that good dome behind gave me a headache. That would actually be a great way for him to make some money. He could teach a class on how to eat pussy so good that a bitch will never leave.

"Aries, you cannot be a part of the family."

"Because your dad is a fucking racist!"

"He's not racist. His wife is black and so are his kids."

"Y'all are half."

"Regardless, I consider myself a black woman, not mixed, okay? And does he prefer people who have some Russian blood being a part of the family? Yes, he does, but he still brings in black people. Pharaoh didn't have any Russian in him."

"Fuck that nigga. And so what you saying? What's the criteria if he ain't a racist prick?"

"He only brings in people that he feels can be an asset to him, to the family, Aries."

"I'm a got damn asset, aight?"

"Okay, what could you help with?" I folded my arms, ready to hear this.

The only thing Aries could do was cook up dope and rob niggas on the streets. The family didn't deal with petty crimes like that. We pulled off shit that would get you jailed for two consecutive life sentences. My dad had a right to be choosy, because allowing the wrong person to oversee something could take us all down.

"I know how to cook."

"Baby, what part of our operation deals with trap houses and shit? You need to go work for Gang or something, he could use you."

"I could do something for TQ, hit him up for me."

"Aries—"

"Hit the nigga up!"

"Okay, okay."

I knew for a fact that TQ would laugh in my face and have me admitted to a psych ward. Aries couldn't do shit for us, and he needed to realize that. On the other hand, I wanted to see my man win, and maybe if I did present him in a certain way, my father or brothers would be willing to let him lend a helping hand for some cash.

As I was thinking, he pushed me onto my back, lifted my skirt, and yanked my thong down. I propped myself up on my elbows, and watched him push his face into my center, giving me the tongue lashing of a lifetime. I threw my head back in ecstasy, while rubbing his fresh fade. It was crazy how we always went from fighting to him sucking the life out of my clit. Yeah, I would figure out a way to get him on.

CHAPTER FIVE

Britain

I pulled up to the house I bought for Tekeya, because today I had to do some cleaning in that muthafucka. The stunt she pulled that day at the car wash was beyond the last straw for me, and there was no coming back from it. I was tired of dealing with Tekeya and all the drama she came with, and in addition to that, I wanted her completely out of my life by the time Goldie agreed to be my damn girl.

Getting out of my all black Bugatti Chiron, I hit the alarm and walked through the black gate. The big ass house didn't look like much on the outside, but once you entered that muthafucka, it was like a palace. I planned to have this shit fixed to my liking, and maybe I would move in down the line. Right now, I was content with my luxe ass condo though.

Entering the house, I checked the kitchen and saw Tekeya wasn't in there. I then went up to the bedroom, and as I got closer, I heard her singing something like she always did when she was alone in a room. I opened the door, and she snapped her neck to look at me. She stared at me, not sure of what to say as I closed the bedroom door. Visions of me slapping her ass up and down the room invaded my mind, but I quickly shook them.

"Brit—"

"Sit down," I cut her off, moving my dreads from my face.

She did as I asked, and once I was seated on the ottoman, I just stared into her pretty face for a bit. A part of me still had love for her, but most of me couldn't stand her ass anymore. She was always doing too much, and because of who I was, I needed someone who was more chill, like Goldie. I didn't need any negative attention brought on me, and it seemed like Tekeya always caused me problems in public. It was bad enough that I was a Quinton and authorities were already side eyeing me, so I didn't need that extra kick she was attempting to give; especially not in the form of a domestic violence charge.

Secondly, I never really wanted to be with Tekeya like that. As I'd explained to Goldie, getting with her was more of an ego thing, and something that I let go on longer than I should have since I was still able to do what I wanted. But now that I had my eyes on another woman, it was time I ended what we had. It was time that I grew the fuck up and let her know the truth.

"Britain, I'm sorry about the whole police situation, and bringing Angelica up there with me to cause a scene at the car wash," she fidgeted.

"Why did you? I'm curious."

"Because you weren't calling me or texting me, and I felt like you should have been. I caught you cheating on me in front of a park full of people! You humiliated me, Britain! You should have been groveling like no other!"

"You're right in the fact that I shouldn't have been sexing another girl in the same setting as you. And I can't blame you for reacting to something like that the way that you did, because I'm sure it was very embarrassing. But Key, this is nothing new for us. You are always fighting me or another girl, and taking shit too far."

"It's because I love you and I'm fighting for what's mine."

"And I can't get down with that, ma, I really can't. Like I told you at the car wash, I think it's best we go our separate ways. The relationship is toxic, and I'm not happy."

"What can I do to make you happy, Britain?" she got up and walked over to me, before kneeling down.

"Nothing baby, it just ain't meant and you know that. I know you're not happy in this. How could you be?"

"I am because I love being with you and anytime that I am, I'm happy. If you would just give me a chance, I'm sure we could go back to how we used to be," she smiled.

"How was that?"

"What?"

"How did we used to be, Key?"

"We used to love being together all the time. Everything was better, don't you remember?"

"No, I don't remember. What I remember is us only getting along in the bedroom. We were never calm and cool together, because from day one, you felt the need to fight every girl that knew me, and then proceed to fight me. Name one time, more than a day, where we were happy and had no drama."

"Don't do that, Britain." She stood to her feet.

"Don't do what, Key? I'm trying to understand and recall this blissful time we had together that you speak of. Because I just don't remember."

It seemed like I was having some sort of epiphany. I was by no means a faithful nigga, but most nights that I spent with other women were because I didn't feel like coming home to fight Tekeya. There would be times where I was actually being faithful because I'd been too busy to fuck around, and she would still find a reason to fight me, or pop up on some girl and fight her. She only refrained from hitting me for like two months, and that was because my sister Saya whooped her ass for slapping me in front of her. But after those two months, she went right back to nutting the fuck up on me whenever she felt the need to. I could honestly say Tekeya was worse than Dania, and Dania accidentally fought our cousin.

"Because you were fucking around the whole time!" she growled and began taking off on me, like she always fucking did. "And who is your baby mama? I saw her text your phone!!!!!"

"See! See!" I grabbed her wrists. "You can't even have one damn civil conversation without trying to throw hands, Tekeya! I'm calm as fuck right now, yet you feel the need to hit me and shit!"

"Britain—"

"Look, I came to tell you that you need to move up out of here. I'm giving you three months to find somewhere else to live, which in my opinion is more than enough time, ma. After three months, you're out on yo' ass. The relationship is over, and don't claim me or act a fool if you see me out, you got it?" I seethed.

Tears began to well up in her eyes as she moved wildly, trying to get her wrists from my grasp. She wasn't strong enough though, so she just looked like a crazy person. I finally got tired, so I threw her down onto the bed before leaving out of the bedroom. You could hear her screaming and crying from here to Timbuktu.

Getting back into my car, I rested my head on the headrest with my eyes closed. I felt like a weight had been lifted off of my shoulders. And once Tekeya moved out, and Goldie agreed to be exclusive, life would be all good.

My phone buzzed, and I looked down to see it was Goldie, prompting a smile to creep across my face.

Baby Mama: *Where are you? Let's go eat.*

Me: *On my way.*

Tekeya Mitchell

Once I was able to stop crying long enough to get off the bed, I grabbed my phone to dial my best friend, Angelica, so she could come over. I needed to talk to her, and have her make me feel better about what had just happened. Things these days just seemed to be getting worse and worse for me, and I just couldn't deal with it.

"Hello?"

"Come over, please," I sniffled.

"Key, what happened?"

"Just come over, and hurry up, okay?"

"Okay, I'm inside Brother's Deli, did you want anything from here?"

"Just get me whatever you get." I disconnected the call and plopped backwards onto the bed.

I felt like crying some more, but I didn't want my eyes being too puffy when Angelica got here. In order to do that though, I needed to stop thinking about Britain and him leaving me. I loved that man more than I loved myself, and anything else that surrounded me. I would walk in front of a train for him, but none of that mattered. And because he'd done me so wrong, he'd caused me to make some mistakes myself, and now I was paying for it.

After lying there staring up at the ceiling fan for twenty minutes straight, I heard the doorbell ring. Wishing it was him coming back to apologize, but knowing it wasn't, I got up and plodded down the stairs to go answer the door. I let Angelica in, and we went into the kitchen to get ourselves a bottled water, before taking the food to the back patio to eat. I was gonna miss this house.

"Why were you crying, Key? Do I need to beat someone's ass?" Angelica smacked her thin lips.

I chuckled at my friend because her ass couldn't fight for shit, but she stayed ready. Angelica would never back down from any bitch, even knowing that she was gonna get her ass whooped. She just wasn't a punk, and nothing would make her cower. I loved that about her, but I just wished she actually had the hands to back up that mouth of hers.

"He left me."

"You mean officially? Because he hasn't even moved into this house he bought you almost a year ago."

"Yeah, officially. He said the words and everything. And speaking of the house, he's giving me three months to get the hell out of it."

"So he can move his baby's mother in?" she bit into her sandwich.

"Yes. I don't even know who the hoe is that has his baby though. That's just how sneaky he is, so I'm not surprised he has a child out there. I just wish I could find out who she is. When I ask around, niggas act like they don't know what I'm talking about."

"It looks like you guys have more shit in common than I thought," she shook her head.

"You got a cigarette?" I asked, ignoring her statement.

"Key, you—"

"Just give me the cigarette. You know I have to smoke after eating, so hand me one, please."

"Does Britain know?" She handed me a cigarette and her lighter, before going back to eating her sandwich. Angelica was always a slow ass eater, which is why I hated going out to dinner with her.

"No he doesn't know, I have to wait a little bit until I tell him, Ange, I told you that." I took a pull on the cigarette.

"Key, you need to tell him you're pregnant, because if he finds out on his own, there will be hell to pay. I don't know what I would do if I were to lose you."

A tear slipped out of my eye as I listened to Angelica speak. I was pregnant, but not by Britain. Because he was never around me and always up to some bullshit, I found comfort in a friend. That friend and I both shared some anger towards two of the Quintons, so we bonded over that. We bonded a little too much and ended up sleeping together as our own secret revenge, and now I was pregnant. The problem was, I couldn't pin the baby on Britain because he hadn't touched me in months. The last time we had sex was about five months ago, so the timetable wouldn't match up at all.

"You're not gonna lose me. I just need to get him to fuck me and all will be well."

"How though? He moved out, and your baby daddy is dead, so it's not like he can come protect you."

My friend, Peel, fucked around and got killed. I wasn't sure by whom, because no one was about that life to kill someone of his status. Killing anyone associated with Gang was like a death sentence, so I wasn't sure who would put their life on the line like that. The only person who would do such a thing would have to be higher in rank than them, which pointed the finger at a Quinton. *What if Britain found out he fucked me and killed him?* I wondered. The thought made me queasy.

"Peel couldn't protect me against Britain anyway." I blew smoke out as I stared off into the distance.

"You need to turn over a new leaf in order to get on his good side, Key. Once you have him around you, and calm, you can get him to sleep with you. But how are you gonna get him to do it with no protection? You told me he always straps up."

"I will figure something out, but while I'm doing that, we need to figure out who exactly his baby mama is. And once I do, I'm straight killing that bitch."

"What if it's the girl he was fucking at the park that day?" she quizzed and balled up her sandwich paper.

"No way, she was just some pussy he met at the park."

"But you said you didn't find a condom wrapper in his car or the pants he wore that day. Also, he was watching her the whole time, Key. And while you were making his plate, they were smiling all in each other's faces. In addition to that, she is clearly cool with two of his brothers' girlfriends. I'm telling you I think that bitch is the one."

I hadn't peeped all the stuff Angelica had, but what she was saying made a lot of sense. Britain was acting funny that whole time we were there, and it looked like his mind was elsewhere the whole time. And Jamie told me Britain snatched ole girl up angrily when he saw them dancing. Yeah, I was pretty sure I found my murder victim.

"Well that bitch has got it coming then." I took another pull of the cigarette.

"If you can't get Britain to sleep with you, you need to make him pay for what he's done to you, Key. He shouldn't be allowed to live his life happily while you're miserable."

"I agree. I'm just scared to make an enemy out of him."

"The Quintons run the East Coast, but I'm sure we'd be fine in the Midwest somewhere," she chuckled.

"You'd move with me?"

"Of course. But before we leave, we need to make sure Britain suffers."

Matikah

A couple days later…

"Lendsey move, I have to go," I giggled as he hugged me tightly from behind, kissing on my neck.

"You'd rather go to that job than hang out with me?"

"Of course not, baby, but this is my first day, and I cannot miss it. Are we still on for tonight?"

"Hell yeah we are. I can't wait to celebrate with you for passing that test. My shorty is smart, and she got skills." He rubbed up and down the front of my body, groping my breasts in the process.

"Stop before you get too turned on, Len," I moaned, knowing I was talking more about myself.

He turned me to face him, and then kissed my lips gently.

"I love you, shorty, and this second chance will not be regretted."

"I know," I nodded.

***

I made it to Isabetta's Massage Parlor and Spa, and smiled after parking my car. I've waited forever for this moment, and it was finally here. I can't tell you how long I've wanted to do waxes and massages.

This was just the beginning, however, because once I got my name out there, I would have my own shop like Isabetta.

Grabbing my purse, I got out of the car and headed inside. I was greeted by Isabetta, and then she took me to the back to show me the room I would be working out of. It was so big, and I wanted to jump up and down when I saw my name, and a copy of my beauty license framed on the wall.

"How do you like it?" she asked with a smile.

"I love it. It's actually much nicer than I had imagined. And thank you again for giving me a chance."

"No, thank you for coming here. I've seen your work, and it feels good to have a well-trained employee here. There are four other girls you will need to meet, and then I will show you around some more."

"Great."

Not long after that, three girls showed up and introduced themselves. Only two of them were welcoming, but one, Isyss, was a bit standoffish. I think she was upset because she was the type of person who didn't like new people. She must've hated having competition, and if so, she was right to be upset because I was very good at what I did.

After getting to know the girls a tiny bit, Isabetta showed me the product line containing lotions, ingrown hair serums, and other products that we were to push while working on a client. The more she told me, the more excited I became. Once we were done with that, she allowed me to go to my room to familiarize myself with everything in it.

"I told you I was coming today!" I heard a familiar voice yell.

"Calm down, it's not a big deal. Annalise will be done in about forty minutes, and she can take you then," I heard Isabetta respond. "I told you about showing up unannounced, you need to make an appointment. Yes, umm, Annalise is the only one available."

"I don't have that kind of time!"

I stepped out to see what was going on just because I was nosey, and stopped in my tracks when I saw it was Dania acting a damn fool.

"Matikah, you know how to do facials, right? It includes a neck massage," Isabetta turned to me.

"Yes, but—"

"Please take her before I kill her," Isabetta walked up and whispered. "It's just a facial and then an upper back exfoliation."

"Perfect," Dania smiled, not knowing what Isabetta had just said to me, but happy to see me.

"I wasn't exactly prepared to do any facials, but sure, why not," I sighed. I really didn't want to work on her, but I could see Isabetta needed the help and I wanted to impress her. I was just happy I didn't have to give her a Brazilian wax.

"Great, thanks, Matikah. Something nice will be in your paycheck." She patted my shoulder and walked back to the front to speak with Dania, who had her eyes on me, smirking.

I went into the room to pull out what I would need, and as I was doing so, Dania walked in. I smoothed down the massage bed, and changed the height to fit me comfortably. She just stared me down the whole time, expressionless. I felt like the side of my face was burning from her gazing so damn hard.

"I will leave you so that you can get undressed; only the top," I said, breaking through the awkward silence.

"No, no need to leave." She dropped her purse in the chair, blocking the door.

I inhaled sharply as she removed her white t-shirt, and then unhooked her bra. She kept her eyes on me as she slid it down her arms, and I rolled my eyes at the tattoo of my nigga's name on her breast. *This is so weird*, I thought. She chuckled, obviously knowing what I'd rolled my eyes at, and then laid down on the bed faced down.

"I need you to lie on your back so that I can do your face first, Dania."

"I want you to take care of my upper back first."

I declined to respond as I pinned my hair up into a bun. I washed my hands good, and then took some of the body acne cleanser to begin exfoliating her upper back. She had no acne on it, and I guess it was because she came here to make sure she stayed blemish free. After scrubbing it down, I cleaned it off and began massaging the moisturizer into her back. Am I really massaging my boyfriend's crazy side chick? This can't be life.

"Let me know if I'm hurting you," I said, even though I couldn't care less.

"No one can hurt me as bad as Lendsey did." I didn't respond. "He used to care for me like he cares for you now. We always spent a lot of time together, and we had a lot of fun. I can't say I blame you, Lendsey is a charmer and phenomenal in bed. A girl can't help but to fall in love with him. I get sad just thinking about all the nights we shared. Enjoy the time you have with him before it ends."

"It won't end."

"That's what I thought."

"We are different, Dania, and you know that. Your love for Lendsey was unrequited."

"Now it is, but it didn't used to be that way. He used to be really good to me, and used to act like he couldn't live without me," she giggled. "I used to cook for him, I used to—"

"Used to, used to, used to. Do you know what those two words mean? It means that it doesn't happen anymore." I massaged her harder due to my anger. "I'm sorry that you can't get over him, but you're not gonna convince me that you and I are the same because we aren't. You were something he stuck his dick in and nothing more. You know damn well that I mean more than a nut to him. Instead of spending money here, you need to save up and have that tattoo removed."

"Just finish your fucking job so I can go!" she snapped.

That's what the fuck I thought, bitch.

Rhys

Because I'd been so busy handling niggas for my father, and spending any free time I had with my daughter, I'd neglected to come pick my money up from my mother. I wasn't hurting for it, but I did a job and I was to be paid. My sister and mother sometimes tried to get freebies, and I wanted to make sure they understood that I would be compensated for my dangerous ass work.

Walking into my parents' home, I went straight to my mother's office to let her know I was here for my money.

"I will get it from the safe once I finish this phone call, baby," she whispered. I sighed heavily before getting up to give her some privacy.

Entering the guest bedroom, I walked to the bathroom because a nigga had just drunk a whole bunch of water and had to piss like a race horse. Every afternoon I drank a gallon of water, so for a couple hours afterwards, it would have me pissing every two seconds. When I opened the door to the restroom, I saw the call girl that I'd saved a couple weeks ago, stepping out of the shower. Her body looked even better under the bright ass lights in the bathroom.

"Shit, I'm sorry." I closed the door back, a bit ashamed that I'd stood there staring for some time.

A few moments later, she came out of the bathroom wearing a

towel. Her brown hair was drenched and sticking to her neck. She was so damn pretty, and even prettier right now because her makeup wasn't on.

"You can go ahead and use the bathroom now," she replied, avoiding eye contact with me. Ain't like plenty of niggas hadn't seen her body before, so I wasn't sure why she was all bashful now.

"Thanks."

I relieved myself, then came out of the bathroom to see her spreading lotion on her sexy legs. She had on a black dress, but it wasn't a go out to the club type of dress. It looked like something you would wear to the movies or some shit. I watched her for a little bit, then cleared my throat to make myself known.

"Why are you showering at 6pm in the evening? Got work?" I questioned. I don't know why I felt inclined to talk with her. I usually didn't socialize with my mother's employees.

"No, I don't have any clients today. I went to the gym, so I had to shower afterwards."

"Why here? Why you ain't at the hotel?"

"Your mother offered for me to stay here for a little bit until I find a place. She said staying at a hotel is unsafe, and I guess I agree."

"Well I'm sure you have more than enough money to live in your own shit, right?"

"I do," she nodded. It was quiet for a few moments as she combed through her hair.

"You hungry?"

She looked to me, and stared for a little bit before saying, "Ye-yeah, I am."

"Come on." I walked towards the door with her following me.

"Rhys!" I heard my mother calling my name.

"Right here, you got my bread?" I quizzed.

"Yes, here." She handed me a leather bag full of cash, while glancing back and forth between Indiya and I.

"Let me get my purse," Indiya broke the silence.

"Should I be charging you?" my mother asked.

"No, Ma, we're just getting something to eat. All the pussy being thrown at me and you think I'm gonna pay for it? And can't the girl do things without having to charge?"

"Okay, Rhys, just making sure." She walked off right when Indiya came out, ready to leave.

We left out and I opened the door of my Aston Martin for her to get in. I then placed the money in my trunk, hidden under a black piece of board, before getting in on the driver's side.

"This is a beautiful car, Rhys," she smiled, as she looked around it using her eyes.

"It's okay," I smirked, making her chuckle. "What do you have a taste for?"

"Surprise me."

"Is there anything you don't like?"

"Not really, but I'm obsessed with Russian food," she smiled.

"You have any Russian ancestry?" I asked as I sped down the street.

"Yes, my father is Russian. My name is Indiya Nikolaev."

"Damn, for real? So we have something in common. Your mother is black I'm guessing?" I glanced over at her, and then back at the road.

"Yes, she is."

I ended up taking her to Verenich, an upscale Russian restaurant on Huntington Avenue in Allston. My family owned it, and it was the best Russian food in Boston. Even people who had no Russian blood loved it here, and anytime my family and I got together, we would eat here.

"Why is your last name Quinton?" she asked once we were seated. I made sure to request a secluded area because I didn't care to deal with any dick riders this evening. I heard people came here in hopes of running into someone from my family.

"That's my father's last name."

"It's not Russian though."

"I know, he changed his name to Stony Quinton, because he said his birth-name was too Russian. He wanted to fit in better and shit, I guess."

"Makes sense. People see my last name and assume all sorts of things about me. Especially because I'm named after a South Asian country," she grinned.

"That's like my little brother, Britain. If it were up to my father, he wouldn't have that name, but he and my mom made a deal that she could name the boys and he could name the girls. Saya is the only one he had any input on."

"I always wondered why you guys didn't have Russian first names. People ask me why my first name is Indiya all the time when they find out I'm part Russian."

"I'm sure that can get confusing, for sure. I like your name though. Sometimes I wish my name showed my Russian roots, shit even my black roots. Looking at my name, you have no idea what I am."

"True, but I think that's better. People can't judge you ahead of time, like for job interviews."

"I don't think I will be going on any, anytime soon, but thank you for trying to make me feel better, I appreciate it."

"No problem," she chuckled.

We both ordered the Zharkoye, which is like stew, and had the honey cake for dessert. Everything was so damn good, and had a nigga stuffed like a muthafucka. Surprisingly, Indiya held good conversation, and I really enjoyed the time we spent at the table. I hadn't enjoyed myself with a woman since Summer, and that was pretty much over I guess.

"Are you taking me back to your parents' home?" she asked as I drove away from the restaurant.

"Where else would you like to go?"

"Can I come to your house?"

I stared at her for a bit at the red light and said, "I don't see why not."

I got to my condo in no time, thanks to this fast ass whip, and after I removed the money from my trunk, I opened the door for Indiya. We made it up into my condo, and I hurriedly snatched up the Barbie dolls that my shorty had left all over my living room. Indiya laughed as I cleaned up.

"Sorry about that."

"No, it's cute," she smiled and sat down on the couch, crossing her sexy legs in the process.

"Thirsty? I can make you a drink, after I put this shit up, of course."

"Some wine is fine, thank you."

I put Bryleigh's dolls in her room, placed my money in my safe, and then went to the kitchen to get some wine for us both. When I returned, she had her shoes off, and was standing by the window looking down. She appeared to be in deep thought, and I almost didn't want to disturb her.

"Here you go," I handed over the wine.

"Oh, thanks. You live alone?"

"Now I do."

"What happened?"

"My girlfriend and I decided to go our separate ways, that's all."

"May I ask why?"

"She didn't trust me, and I guess I didn't do a good job to make her trust me, so she ended the relationship. And she thought I was a very angry person. Said she was scared of me."

"You seem like a good guy, and you don't seem temperamental at all."

"I guess I am, in certain lights, but you can't spend your life trying to get someone to see the good in you. After a while, you get tired of attempting to sell yourself to someone who isn't interested in your product."

"Makes sense."

"How did you get into this business? I'm sure you could be doing something else."

"You think so?" she sipped her wine.

"I do."

"I moved here when I was twenty-one, and had no money or anything. I tried working jobs here and there, but they would always figure out I was an illegal citizen and threaten to report me. Then I met Saya, and she hooked me up with her business."

"Illegal? I thought your mother was black?"

"She's African, I'm sorry." African, no wonder she was so damn beautiful.

"Really? How did she meet your Russian father?"

She snickered and said, "My father travels a lot, especially to Africa. During one of his trips, he met my mom and they spent a year together. She got pregnant with me, and everything was good. She traveled to Russia with my father, where she died from some sort of infection. Turns out she wasn't given the best medical care upon giving birth." She stared out of the window as she spoke.

"Damn, so you never met her?"

"Not when I was old enough to have memories, no. She was great though, my father says."

"Does your family know what you do?"

"No, hell no. My father would murder me, I'm sure."

"Yeah, Russian fathers are nothing nice when they get upset. I know that firsthand, but I won't let anything happen to you."

"No?"

"Didn't I prove that when I shot that old fart back in the hotel?"

"You did, and I appreciate that," she chuckled, and set the wine on the windowsill, before moving in closer to me.

Before she even made it to me, I lifted her up, letting her wrap her legs around my waist. Taking her to my bedroom, I dimmed the light with one hand while still holding her up with the other. I then laid her down on the bed, and began to remove my clothes. She pulled her dress off as she watched me, and my dick got so damn hard immediately. Her body was one of the sexiest I had ever seen, and I could just look at it all day. Russian and African, what a beautiful combination.

She wasn't wearing a bra, so I climbed onto the bed and pulled her panties down while sucking her beautiful nipples. She caressed my baldhead as I sucked for dear life. I've wanted to do this to her since the first time I saw her. They just sat up so perfectly.

"You know this is not why I asked you to get something to eat."

"I know," she nodded. "I haven't slept with a person that I wanted to sleep with in a while, so don't think you're taking advantage of me.

You're doing me a favor."

"I am?" I smiled.

"Yes," she whispered before I slipped my tongue into her mouth.

For a few moments, I just kissed her and let my hands rub all over her flawless body. Her soft skin felt so good under me, and I couldn't wait to be inside of her. Standing up on my knees, I grabbed a condom and rolled it down slowly as she watched.

"You're so big," she bit her lip.

I laid down between her legs, and positioned myself at her opening. Sliding inside, her pussy was nothing like what I'd expected. I thought it would be loose or worn, but the shit was virgin tight, warm, and just straight up perfection. She was right to be charging for this shit.

"Mmm, shit," she moaned.

I continued gliding in and out of her until her body jerked lightly from exploding. Her soft moans only made my dick harder as I continued to gently pound her spot. Her small hands rubbed up and down my back as I humped her in a circular motion, causing us both to moan out. Damn.

Once she came again, I put her on all fours, and slid inside her from behind. Gripping her small waist, I rammed her pussy like crazy until she was spilling her nectar on my rod again.

"Uuuh, aaah, uuuh, Rhys, baby!" she called out as I went to town on her pussy. I was fucking it like I hated it. "Uhh, uuuh," she cried out, balling the sheets up in her fists, and clenching her teeth.

Seeing her pretty face knot up in pleasure as she looked back at me, and the feeling of her wetting my dick again caused me to release, filling the condom up. Pulling out, I went to flush the condom, and grabbed two warm soapy towels for us to clean up with. Once we were done, I went to drop them in the hamper. Climbing into my bed, she snuggled up to me and laid on my chest.

"Aye, don't take this the wrong way, but I didn't expect your pussy to be so good and tight. That was definitely one of the top five I've ever had."

"It is an insult, but I'm not easily disturbed. And babies come out of our vaginas, so do you honestly think you niggas' dicks can stretch anything out?"

"I didn't think of it that way. But anyway, your pussy is top notch, ma, I see why you charge for it."

She got up, straddled my lap, and then said, "That'll be a grand." I stared at her like she was nuts, then she burst into laughter. "I'm kidding. You know I've never had an orgasm until tonight."

"For real? Damn. I feel bad for your pussy."

"Yeah, most of my clients are little dick old men who don't know what they're doing. I've had a couple of young guys, but they're just as bad because they all cum quickly. And before I became an escort, I only had two boyfriends. One could barely keep it up, and the other never lasted long."

"Well, I'm happy to be the first, I guess." I rubbed her thighs, and then up her flat stomach before cupping her perfect titties. "These are beautiful."

"Thank you. They're real too."

"I know. They're not big enough to be fake."

"I guess that's a compliment."

"It is. Come here." I pulled her down into my chest, and dipped my tongue back into her mouth.

Shorty was dope as fuck.

CHAPTER SIX

A few days later…

"I was finally able to get the results," Huxley, the scientist nigga my dad worked with said.

I'd hired him to get the brick used to clock Kimberlyn tested for fingerprints. Hopefully, the person was dumb enough to not have used gloves. I mean they were stupid enough to leave the damn bloody brick at the scene. That's like stabbing someone and leaving the knife in.

"About time, nigga, it's been forever!"

"I know, TQ. It's just hard to get into the lab without people getting suspicious. I had to find the perfect time to—"

"I really don't care. What the fuck came back so I can murk their asses, man?"

"The prints on the brick belong to a Monica Jordan."

"Monica Jordan?" I frowned, trying to think of who I knew with the name Monica.

I honestly was expecting it to be some bitch I busted down in the past, but I was happy as hell I was wrong. I mean, if this Monica bitch was someone I'd slept with, she was one of the girls I didn't remember. I only remembered a few though, so I guess that wouldn't be too much of a negative thing on her part.

"Yes, she works as a secretary for Schroder and Faire law firm."

"Monica—" that's when it hit me.

Gang used to mess with a bitch named Monica who was a receptionist or some shit at a law firm. I remember because when he got in some legal trouble, she helped him out with a few things. She was like logging into systems to see what evidence they had on him, or something illegal as fuck like that. Clearly he was still fucking with the girl, because she felt the need to attack mine. I just hoped he had a new bitch in mind because Monica was a dead one.

"Thanks, Hux," I responded as all kinds of shit went through my damn mind. "Aye, do you have her address or anything?"

"I just have her work address here," he replied.

"I'll take it."

***

I sat outside of the law firm, waiting for this bitch to get off because I was beyond ready to kill her ass. I wouldn't feel bad afterwards, because she knew what she was doing when she decided to fuck with a person so closely affiliated with me. Kimberlyn was my shorty, and every muthafucka with a brain knew that she was off limits in every way possible. She wasn't to be bothered, talked to, fucked with, or anything else that would upset me. She was above all the hoes who had interest in me, and too good to be dealing with the random niggas floating around Boston. Her life was different now, and the only thing muthafuckas should've been doing in her presence was bowing the fuck down.

I watched as Monica switched to her car in a tight fitting dress. Her body was very healthy, and very sexy, but too bad she wouldn't be able to use it again. Just looking at her walking to her car as if she hadn't done something despicable, had me seething. She cranked up her Toyota Avalon, and once she sped out, so did I in my 1995 black Jeep with Maine plates.

Making sure not to follow too closely, I finally made it to her condo in Mission Hills. She was living well, which had me wondering if she'd paid for all this herself, or if Gang did. The sun had already set, so it was slightly dark outside. She climbed out of her car, and went to the back of it to open her trunk. I slowly drove down her street, going the opposite way her car was pointing, with my window cracked.

PHEW! PHEW!

As soon as she closed her trunk, I sent two silent shots into her head. One entered the side, and the other into her cheek. Her blood and brain matter splattered onto her back windshield, and the car parked behind hers, front windshield. I didn't speed off, I just continued down the street as if nothing happened. She would be there for some hours before anyone noticed because no one was outside, and this was a fairly quiet neighborhood, and that was a fairly quiet assault.

On the way to the warehouse, I felt satisfied, and I knew I would finally be able to have a good night's sleep. Before, I would toss and turn, or stay up until the wee hours of the morning just angry. The disrespect was at an all time high, which ruined my sleep pattern. But now that ole girl was dead, I was all good. All I had to do now was torch this whip at the warehouse with the pistol inside, and then go home.

***

When I walked into my condo, Kimberlyn was still awake, working on her computer. She looked really into it, and her facial expressions were hilarious. I took my hoodie off, and walked over to her and kissed her lips.

"What you working on?"

"New project for class. I'm getting a headache already," she exhaled.

"It'll be worth it once you graduate and can charge people to make their websites."

"I know. I've done a couple people's blogs and sites for small fees, but this degree will give me reason to up my prices."

"I know that's right," I smirked.

I reached across her and lifted her shirt to look at her stomach. It was bulging now, and the shit was kind of cool to see. A fucking person was in there, which was wild. I kissed it a couple times, and she leaned back to allow me more access.

"How was your day? I made quesadillas for you," she caressed my fade.

"Thank you. It was great in a sense. I caught the person who assaulted you, a girl named Monica."

"Monica?" she bucked her eyes, prompting me to sit up.

"Yeah, you know her?"

"Yes I know her! She was always a bitch to me whenever she would hang out with Gang and I. I knew she liked him, but he swore she didn't."

"She was fucking with him for years," I said, making her frown in confusion.

"He told me she was just a friend."

"I'm sure she was a fuck buddy."

"Did you make up with your dad?" she straddled my lap, changing the conversation. I was happy to see that she didn't care that Gang was playing her.

"Nah ma, and I don't think I will anytime soon."

"What did he do?"

"Just know that my father only had kids to secure his legacy and nothing else. He doesn't see us the same way normal fathers see their kids. We're more like pieces in his game, and he only needs us for one thing. He doesn't really care what's going on in our lives, as long as it doesn't affect business."

"He doesn't love you?" she caressed my face.

"He loves what we can do for him. Quinton Crime Family is his child, and all he cares about is making sure it prospers and reigns supreme."

"Well, I love you."

"I know, shorty, and I love you too. I won't be like that with our baby."

"I know you won't. I can't wait to bring your baby here, Tarenz," she whispered.

"Me neither."

She eased her tongue into my mouth, before I stood up to carry her to the shower. I was about to celebrate my disposal of Monica, and then take my frustration with my father out on that pussy.

Jayce Lincoln

One week later…

"Make this shit quick, I have to meet with TQ. I told you it ain't good for me to meet you in person anyway. That nigga has eyes everywhere."

"Calm down, this is my muthafuckin city. I'm tired of niggas acting like they don't know," Gang snapped as he stood up from the round table we were sitting at.

He called me earlier and told me that we needed to talk. When I initially started being cool with this nigga, I told him it wasn't a good idea for us to be seen together. Usually I would've denied his meeting invitation, but when he said I could come to his crib, I obliged. No one would see us in this huge ass shit, so I didn't have much to worry about.

I started linking up with Gang because TQ and the family weren't giving me the respect I felt I deserved. I used to be a big part of that shit, but now I was nothing more than one of the young runners. I was a big dog but these niggas were treating me like a toy poodle. At first I wasn't tripping because they were right about me being too depressed to handle anything, but I felt I had proved myself enough to be put back in the game. I wasn't meant to just assist the brothers whenever they needed me, which was rare. I was meant to have my own area within Quinton Crime Family like they did.

TQ and I grew up together, and since I was a troubled child, his father, Stony, took me in. He didn't groom me as much as he did his own offspring, but he showed me enough. As I got older, I was given more responsibilities, and was somewhat like his sixth kid. I had money, cars, women, houses, and everything; I was living life. I had even eventually found a shorty to settle down with named Sadie.

Like a typical man, though, I entertained other females simply because I could. I was handsome, rich, and had a portion of the reigns over the East Coast. Women were ridiculous when it came to the Quinton brothers and I. There wasn't a place we could walk into where a woman wasn't willing to fuck and suck us right then and there. There was nothing that these women wouldn't do to get close to us, so it was hard to just turn the other cheek. And these weren't no ugly bitches either, they were bad as fuck! We all indulged, but I was the only one tied down.

To make a long story short, I ended up becoming too involved with this shorty named Jennifer. She was fine as fuck, and the pussy was almost comparable to my wife's. Like always, she took the relationship more seriously than I did, so when I tried to break it off for a new piece of ass, she went nuts. She threatened my wife and me on countless occasions, but I never took her seriously. I mean, would you? I was Jayce Lincoln and she'd be a fool to try and touch me, let alone my wife. I was wrong, sadly, because she ran up on my wife at the nail shop and shot her right in the head. Yeah, the bitch was crazy enough to do it in a nail shop full of people. She walked out like it was nothing, and got arrested about ten minutes later.

When that happened, I lost my mind in a sense. All I did was drink and snort a little cocaine here and there. I wanted to die, but I was too much of a coward to off myself. Contrary to popular belief, I was slightly religious, so my Christian faith had me thinking I would go to hell if I killed myself, so I couldn't do it. The day my wife died was one of the worst days of my life, and a huge turning point for me. I haven't been the same since, but now I was determined to become a winner again.

"Are you fucking listening?!" Gang barked, snapping me from my thoughts.

"Yeah, now what the fuck you say?" I chuckled because I had no way out of the fact that it was obvious I hadn't been listening.

"I said we gon' have to take out ya boy."

"TQ?" I frowned.

"Yeah man, he's gone too far. I know for a fact that he popped Peel, and I know he killed Monica too."

"Why would he kill Monica?"

I could guess why he killed Peel. I mean, TQ was fucking his girl, and maybe Peel found out. I don't know and I didn't give a fuck, which is why when Gang asked me if TQ was smashing Hayden, I acted as if I didn't know. I didn't care to be a part of these lovers' quarrels. I was more interested in finding out why he murked Monica. We didn't talk like we used to because all he did was work, or spend all his time with Kimberlyn. If he wasn't flying to another state, holding a meeting, or importing, he was out to dinner, at the movies, or traveling with his shorty. Usually, I would be happy for him, but I just couldn't be; it irritated me.

"Because she attacked Kimberlyn."

"It was her?" I sat up.

"Yeah, nigga. I heard her talking on the phone to her friend one night. I approached her about it and she just sold me some sob story about how I'd drove her to this. Only reason I ain't fuck her up was because Kimberlyn lived."

"So then what's the problem? I mean if Kimberlyn had have died you would have handled her anyway."

"Monica was *my* bitch, and him killing her is disrespectful to me. Ain't no other man supposed to reprimand my bitch, and you know that!"

"I guess I feel what you're saying. But if you want my help, you need to hold up your end of the deal. I want forty percent of the empire."

"Well, now that Peel is dead, I need a new right-hand man anyway. But he only got twenty-five."

"I'm not him, so I want forty. I will take over all of his responsibilities, and help you run things much smoother than he did, I'm sure."

He stared at me with his fingers clasped for a little bit before looking off.

"You got a deal, if you can find another way for us to continue to get product using Quinton connections without TQ. He's the direct link, and without him, the whole East Coast will dry up, not just Boston," he explained. "And if that happens, every kingpin from North Carolina to Maine will be on my head."

"I said I would help you out, right? If anybody knows how the Quinton Crime Family works, it's me. I used to be a big part of the shit for heaven's sake. We just have to make it clean so that his family won't come after us, especially his brothers. Rhys is like a 007 agent."

"I know. I think we're capable."

"Same."

"Well then, let's shake on it," he smirked, reaching his hand across the table. "Do you think Kimberlyn would be willing to give me a chance once he's gone?"

"I don't know, shorty's head is pretty gone, especially now that she's got his baby inside of her."

"Maybe we just have to get ride of that too, then."

Goldie

"I can barely sit down good," I frowned as I rode in the passenger seat of Britain's fresh ass Bugatti.

The car was beautiful and fast as hell. I felt like *that* bitch riding shotgun in such an expensive car, and next to such a fine ass nigga. I smiled as I thought about it, bobbing my head to "My Flag" by The Game.

"That didn't stop your ass from spending my money and walking to every damn store in the mall, shorty," Britain turned the music down a little, smiling at me.

"It was stuff I really needed, that's why," I grinned.

He'd just taken me shopping, and I was up in all the high-end stores picking out shit I'd seen but couldn't buy before. I wasn't one of those bitches who played shy and pretended like I didn't want to spend a nigga's money. I liked nice things but couldn't afford them, so if a nigga I'm fucking offers to buy it for me, then why not? It's not like I was using him, because I wasn't, I really liked Britain. I liked him probably more than I actually should have. But niggas like him enjoyed spending money on their women, so who was I to stop him? Especially when I knew he had more than enough for me to get a Louis bag or two.

"You ain't need none of the shit you got. You only wanted it."

"Very true, but still, I can barely sit because my bottom half is sore as fuck."

"You shouldn't be surprised; you know how I get in the bedroom, shorty."

"I do know, and it's worth it." I rubbed his hand, which sat on the gear shift.

I loved the way his big, strong hands looked. The tattoos on his wrist accompanied by the iced out watch, was so sexy to me. Just from his hands, you could tell he was a boss.

"I'm looking to get you up out of there. My dad's assistant said she found a couple of places that she wants us to look at," he said once he pulled in front of my apartment building.

"Britain, I'm fine here, I don't need to move." I unbuckled my seat belt. I didn't mind him buying me things at the mall, but a place to live was too much, I felt. I hadn't even agreed to being his girlfriend yet.

"You were fine *before* you became my girl, Goldie. Now, I can't have you mingling with the regulars."

"The regulars?" I chuckled and sucked my teeth.

"You really don't know who I am, huh? Or my family."

"I do know."

"You know but you don't understand. We're not corner boys, we're not petty criminals—shit, we're not even like Gang. There are certain people we can't socialize with, and that goes the same for anybody we befriend or get close to. And now that you're my girl, people will treat you differently. It sounds like some bullshit, but I put that on everything. You will notice girls are nicer to you, in hopes of getting close to us, and niggas too. The friends you had before you met me are the only true friends you will have. Any girl after that is either trying to leech off of you to get into clubs, get with a rich nigga, or to fuck me and/or my brothers. That's the honest to God truth, ma."

"I guess I hadn't given it too much thought."

I stared out the front windshield, taking in what he'd told me. Before I knew Britain well, I'd only heard of him. They were like celebrities to me and everyone else too. I guess now that I'd become close to him, I'd forgotten all about that.

"Well, I need you to. And like I said, we're getting you up out of this building."

"Okay. And when did I agree to be your girl? I haven't made a decision yet."

"I made it for you. I will be back to get you later on this evening. You want to go to dinner or something?"

"No, I can cook for you. What do you have a taste for?"

"Piroshki, but you don't know how to make that," he gave me the cutest smile, testing me. "It's a Russian dish."

"I know what the fuck it is and I *can* make it, for your information!" I rolled my neck as I grabbed my shopping bags from the back seat.

"Okay, I want it with meat, rice, cheese, and onions. And for dessert, I want Syrniki. And don't call my mama for help either."

"Fuck you, I don't need help. Once you get done eating, you're gonna think I'm from Russia, nigga," I said, making him burst into laughter.

"I will pick up some pizzas from Dirty Water Dough just in case, okay?"

"Bye, nigga. Just text me the name of the dishes."

"Aye, give me a kiss," he grabbed my arm.

I leaned over to caress his cheek while kissing his soft ass lips. My clit was starting to throb, so I pulled away. I needed to go so I could figure out how to make the shit he wanted, and go to the store to get what I needed. After making love with our mouths, I got out of the car and watched him peel down the street. I eyed until I couldn't see him anymore.

Turning around, I felt like I hit a wall, but no, it was just Ethan. Sadly, I had completely forgotten about this nigga. That's just how wrapped up in Britain I was.

"I've been outside your crib all night."

"For what?" I tried to get around him but he blocked me.

"Fuck you think? We haven't talked in a while, and I'm tired of you hitting ignore on me whenever I try to contact you."

"I don't hit ignore. I blocked you months ago, so I don't even know when you call, boo."

"So now you're being a hoe again?" he scoffed.

"I've never been a hoe, you know that, Ethan. Now please move so I can put my shit up, thank you."

I was annoyed by him, but also a little afraid that he would try to hit me again. That shit hurt like hell last time, and the pain lasted for fucking centuries. Also, if Britain saw my face bruised, Ethan would be a dead man. Did I care? Maybe a little bit, but only because I knew him and would hate to see anyone I knew well go into the ground.

"Then what are you doing with the person that was in the car?"

"How do you know that wasn't a home girl?"

"Nah, it wasn't, because you're stepping out the whip with Louis bags and shit. Ain't no friends of yours got that kind of money to be whipping no damn Bugatti, and shopping at stores like that with you."

"In case you haven't heard, Kimberlyn's new boyfriend is very wealthy." I stepped around him, making him turn around to face me.

"So it's true, she really is with TQ."

"She sure is."

"How'd she manage to pull that off? And don't get used to the nice things, he's gonna throw her ass to the side like every other bitch in the past. Y'all hoes kill me. You get with niggas who you know ain't about shit, then be surprised and wanting sympathy when that nigga treats you like scum," he scoffed and pulled a cigarette from behind his ear.

"I guess I should've heeded to the warnings about you, then maybe I wouldn't have wasted my time."

He moved closer to my face and said, "Bitch, I'm the best thing you will ever have. You will never have a nigga like me again, and I'm the best it gets for bitches like you, ma. Yeah, you're pretty as hell, but that's all you got going for you. I mean shit, Kimberlyn is the one with TQ, not you," he chuckled and took a pull on the cigarette before blowing the smoke in my face.

I initially wanted to keep my relationship from him because I didn't want too many people knowing. But now that he was trying to down me, I felt like I had to disclose that information.

"I guess these nice things Britain Quinton bought me don't mean a thing, huh?"

The look on his face was so priceless that I wished I'd had my camera out. He searched my eyes with his for the longest, letting his cigarette burn itself away between his fingertips. A smug expression appeared on my face as I waited for him to let my few words soak into his pitiful ass mind.

"So what, you're just some pussy he's fucking anyway. All them niggas are the same! Just like with me, I only fucked you until I found someone better."

"Then why are you here right now? Why are you constantly begging me to take you back? Why do you sit outside of my house for hours, then get mad when I'm not home, huh?"

"Shut the fuck up!!!!" he hollered so loudly that even the poodle this lady was walking, stopped and looked at Ethan as if it was thinking, *what the fuck*. "Don't you come at me like that, you bitch!!"

"Aye, keep it pushing."

I heard a gun cock, and looked to see my homeboy and neighbor, Owen, holding a gun to Ethan's head. Owen was crazy as fuck, but was super cool. He'd smoked with Matikah, Kimberlyn, and I a couple times, so we did consider him a friend I guess.

"My bad, bro, I—'

"Step," Owen grimaced, tightening his grip on the pistol. It was as if someone had pressed the pause button on my whole street because no one was making noise or moving.

Ethan slowly backed up, and once he was far enough away, he booked it to his car, which was parked a little ways down.

"Thanks, Owen," I smiled.

"No problem. Where has your friend been? Matikah?"

"Oh, she's been busy. Maybe we can all get together and smoke again."

"Yeah, with Kimberlyn too."

"She's pregnant, so probably not," I chuckled.

"Alright, well just hit me up and let me know," he smirked, and then turned around to go back to his place across the street.

I rushed off into my apartment because I still had this dinner to cook, and it needed to be perfect.

What a day…

Lendsey

Off the good tree, and I'm leanin'. You can hear my engine. Girls on my nuts, big Bern been pimpin'.

My brothers, Jayce, and I, plus our women, were being escorted into the back of the club, as "Dope Boy Dance" by Berner played loudly as fuck over the venue. Matikah swayed a little bit to the music as we held hands, going up the winding staircase, which led to the VIP area we were being seated in. Three hostesses immediately came in, carrying buckets filled with ice and juice, and bottles in the other hand. When we went out, we made sure that we had the best of the best liquor in our VIP. Clubs loved to give their house liquor away, but we didn't fuck with that shit. We had multiple bottles of Patrón, Grey Goose, Louis XIII, Pappy Van Winkel, and we even had some Ace of Spades champagne. Everyone planned to get twisted, except Kimberlyn.

Before the bottles were even placed on the table good, we began popping some open. Jayce was staring like a dog who hadn't drank water in ages. That nigga was a drunkard, and I didn't care how many times he claimed he'd sobered up. He'd popped open one of the expensive ass Rip Van Winkle Bourbons, and began taking it to the head. We had four bottles of it, but that shit was $2,000 and not meant to be taken by one greedy ass nigga.

"Slow down, shorty," I whispered into Matikah's ear before kissing it gently.

"You sure you don't want me to be drunk?" she smiled.

"You right, drink up. I want some sloppy ass head tonight."

"I thought I already did a good job," she looked to me with furrowed brows.

"You do, which means if you're drunk, it'll be otherworldly. I don't think you've ever given me head while drunk."

"No, we smoked together once and I did. How was that?"

"Bomb, I could only imagine if you get cross faded," I grinned, thinking about that shit. The head tonight would be crazy between both of us.

"Get ready," she winked.

She refilled her glass with some more Patrón and juice, then slid into my lap to dance to "I'm Up" by Omarion. My shorty was so sexy, and the way she moved her body slowly but still on beat had my dick growing more by the minute. I just sat back, sipped my drink, and continued to get the best lap dance in all of my twenty-four years. The whole club was having a good time, and the environment was turnt as fuck, making the experience that much greater.

"I wanna fuck right now," I pulled her into my chest and whispered into her ear once she was done.

"Gotta wait, boo," she chuckled before standing up. "Going to the bathroom." She walked off with Kimberlyn and Goldie behind her.

Summer wasn't here, but I guess I wasn't surprised since she was for real done with my brother. Everybody was kind of looking at her sideways because we all knew Rhys was being good to her. She was just insecure and I guess the damage done was irreparable. I just think she wasn't over being shot by Lisa's demented ass. We warned Rhys that Lisa was a grizzly bear and not the cub he claimed she was.

"Mr. Quinton," one of the bouncers approached me.

"Yes?"

"There is a woman here wishing to speak with you."

"The fuck, ask who it is. Fuck you coming over here sending messages when you ain't got all the damn details," I snapped. I glanced around his big ass but couldn't see shit as he walked off.

He appeared again from the darkness, walking back up to me. "Her name is Dania Melchior."

"Umm…" I looked over my shoulder to see if Matikah was coming back yet. Rhys and I made eye contact, and he shook his head 'no'. "Tell her we will have to talk another time, thanks."

The bouncer nodded then disappeared again. Matikah and her friends returned only a few moments later, and I was thankful that I'd taken Rhys' silent advice. TQ and Britain just laughed at me because they already knew what I was thinking. Matikah, Goldie, and Kimberlyn went to stand by the balcony to look over the club and dance, so I took that time to fill my glass with straight Louis XIII. I glanced over and saw Jayce making out with two randoms, holding an almost empty bottle of bourbon. *This nigga*, I thought.

"Is Summer budging at all?" I quizzed Rhys. TQ and Britain were looking at him as well, I guess wondering the same thing.

"Nope, and I stopped trying."

"Yeah, maybe that's best. I was getting tired of watching you chase her ass when you ain't even do shit." TQ turned his lip up before downing his glass of Louis XIII, and pouring some Van Winkle into his glass.

"Well, I got tired too. And now she's dating the nigga that I fucked up."

"The one you caught her on a date with?" Britain bucked his eyes and Rhys nodded.

"That's shady. She could've at least got a new nigga to fuck with," I said. "And what about the girl she saw you in the picture with? You still talk to her?"

"Hell nah. Shit, I wasn't talking to her then, but she was just in the right place at the right time and got me caught up. I wasn't even fucking the bitch, and had no plans to either. She didn't understand that though."

"So now you can be on your bachelor shit for us. We can live vicariously through you," Britain grinned, making us laugh.

"Wait, you plan on being a one-woman man?" I snapped my neck to look at him.

"If you and TQ can do it, so can I. And plus, shorty knows how to make Russian food. I tested her ass and she passed, surprisingly," Britain replied.

"Aye, don't compare me to you, nigga, I was never slanging dick like you," TQ munched on some ice.

Rhys, Britain, and I just looked at him like he was crazy because he was lying like a muthafucka. TQ used to give us tips on how to have two girlfriends and shit if we wanted to. He schooled us on all the player shit, like what to say and what not to say to girls so that they wouldn't get the impression that they were our girlfriends if we didn't want them to be. Rhys wasn't really the player type, so it was obvious who taught Britain and I our womanizing ways. Yeah, we tweaked it to our liking as we became men, but TQ was the original. Niggas in my class in high school used to for real look up to him, because he had so many bitches on his dick. He still did, just like the rest of us, but I guess we all were turning over a new leaf.

"Aye, you think they put voodoo on us?" Britain questioned. I knew his ass was low-key twisted already.

"Fuck are you talking about, nigga?" Rhys asked as we laughed.

"Like, how the fuck the same group of friends get us to be in relationships and shit?" He squinted his eyes as if he were pondering the theory.

"Birds of a feather flock together, little bro. They're all alike in one way or another. We were all missing something out of the women we were currently smashing, which is something this group of friends brought to us. It's not voodoo," TQ explained, making Britain and I nod in agreement.

The girls came back over to join us, and we continued to have drinks, talk, and dance. We were all having a good ass time, even Rhys. I was happy to see my brother enjoying himself, despite his situation.

Around 1am, we all decided to leave so we were escorted out the back of the club. As I was waiting for Britain to finish helping Goldie get in so I could help Matikah get in, I heard screaming and the sound of someone running. Looking to my left, I saw it was Dania running up to me at full speed.

"You stupid muthafucka!" She was crying so hard that the black shit on her eyes was staining her cheeks. "Lendsey," she cried out as our security held her back from me.

"Get in the car," I told Matikah, who turned to face me with a frown of confusion. She hesitated while looking at Dania, who appeared to be having a mental breakdown. "Get in." She did as I asked, and I closed the door behind her. "Fuck are you doing, ma?" I made my way over to Dania.

"Let me just talk to you," she sniffled.

"About what?" I touched my security's forearm, letting him know he could release her. As soon as he did, she rushed into me and threw her arms around my neck to hug me tightly.

"I miss you, stop doing this to me!" she sobbed as I tried to peel her arms from around my neck.

"Dania, you're gonna make me do something I don't want to do, shorty. I need you to back off for real and forever." I looked into her face, holding her arms in my grasp.

"No! I'm not going down without a fight! If you choose her, I will end her!" she growled through tears.

I looked at her while shaking my head with sympathy. I then made eye contact with my security, nodded, and then walked back to the truck. On my way, I could hear her screaming and crying at the top of her lungs while being carried to a black van. I tried to save her, but she clearly didn't want to be saved.

CHAPTER SEVEN

Summer

Today, I was taking my baby to Chuck E. Cheese. She loved that place, and since she'd been a good girl in preschool and at home, I decided to surprise her. I loved seeing that pretty smile on her face, even though she was the spitting image of her father.

Speaking of her father, he and I barely talked and I was slowly getting over him, I guess. When we did speak, it was only about Bryleigh and I preferred that. I will be honest and say I was a bit surprised that he hadn't continued to pine for me like he had been doing. But I guess it was for the best, especially now that I was getting closer with Hakim.

The more I got to know Hakim, the more things I liked about him. I enjoyed that he was just a regular guy and not some notorious criminal like Rhys. I didn't have to worry about him going out in the middle of the night to do jobs and shit, which I liked. Being with Hakim felt regular, and that's what I wanted. Dating Rhys Quinton was like being with a celebrity. Everywhere you went, a bitch was either trying to be fake to get close to you, or niggas were trying to be cool with you in hopes of becoming cool with him. It made me feel insecure by being with such an attractive well-known man, and I hated that feeling. I felt like I always had to be dressed perfectly, or looking pristine, because if not, people would wonder why he was with me. Too much was expected of me, and I also didn't like that women stared at him all the time, or told me how fine he was. I was very possessive. Some girls may enjoy that life, but I didn't. I didn't care for the spotlight, and although Hakim was a model, he left his work in Paul's studio.

KNOCK! KNOCK!

I heard a knock at the door, so I knew it was Rhys bringing my baby home. I padded over to answer it, and like always, her hair wasn't combed but she was dressed to the nines.

"I told you that you need to learn to comb hair, Rhys," I scoffed and took her from him.

"I forgot," he shrugged.

"Of course you did."

"What does that mean?"

"Nothing, nothing at all." I sat down, pulling out Bryleigh's hair bucket.

He stood there watching for a bit, before sitting down in the La-Z-Boy chair adjacent to me. We said nothing as I combed Bryleigh's hair, and boy was it awkward. This man and I used to be so in love, and now we couldn't find two words to say to one another; well, two nice words.

"Guess where we're going, Bry?" I asked once I finished her hair.

"Where, Mommy?"

"To Chuck E. Cheese!" I squealed and she jumped into my lap

excitedly.

"Daddy, can you come, please? I need you to hold me in the air to shoot the baskets!" she looked to him. I knew I should've waited until he left to tell her.

"Bry, I don't—"

"Please, Daddy?" she pouted, and I knew she had him. He could never tell her no, and when she pouted, she knew he would for sure give in.

"Okay," he sighed with a smile as he looked at her. Rhys may have been an ugly person internally, but he was as handsome as it got on the outside.

I got up without another word, and went to get my jacket from the back. I really didn't want him to go, but I had no choice. If I told him not to come, Bryleigh would act a damn fool. And if I told her I wasn't taking her, that would break her little heart, so I had to just suck it the fuck up. He was her father and I couldn't completely avoid him.

Chuck E. Cheese was located in Everett, so about fifteen to twenty minutes away. It wasn't too far I guess, but we only came here on occasions. Rhys pulled into the parking lot, hopped out to open my door, and then helped Bryleigh out of the back seat. Once we entered Chuck E. Cheese, we got our hands stamped, and then we supplied Bryleigh with a bucket of coins so she could play games. After running around with her, and helping her win tickets for an hour and a half straight, we sat down to eat pizza. I was actually happy he came because I didn't have to run behind her as much.

I smiled as I thought back to the day we took her to the park. She was about two years old and running everywhere. I was sitting on the bench watching Rhys chase her and play with her, when this pregnant woman with a toddler sat next to me. She told me I was blessed that Bryleigh's father was in her life, because she could barely take her son to the park since she just couldn't chase him like that. I didn't really agree at the time, but now I understood.

"Are you having fun?" I asked Bryleigh as we sat down.

"Yes, I'm happy we can all be together." She bit her pizza slice that was about as big as her. "Come live with us, Daddy."

"I can't, shorty," he exhaled as he watched her eat.

"Mommy can pay all the bills."

We both chuckled at her before he said, "No, it's not because of money, baby. I just can't come home to you guys at the moment." We made eye contact, but I looked away.

Bryleigh finished eating, and then got up to play the game right across from our table. Since we could see her, we both opted out of going over to assist.

"How have you been?" he questioned.

"I've been great, you?"

"You've been great?" he raised a brow.

"Yeah, I have. Why wouldn't I be?"

"Never mind. I guess I'm the only one feeling the effects of the breakup, huh?"

"I guess you are," I sipped my drink as he laughed angrily. "Looks like you were more in love with me than I was with you." He just looked off and nodded his head slowly as if he couldn't believe I'd just said that.

"Still seeing ole boy?"

"His name is Hakim, and yes, I am. We're pretty much boyfriend and girlfriend right now. I thought you should know."

"He's your boyfriend... okay," he nodded slowly again.

"Yes, he's helped me realize that I was never really in love." I didn't believe the shit I was saying, but I was trying to lay it on thick so he would think I was completely over him.

He declined to respond and just got up to go play with Bryleigh.

It started getting dark about an hour later, so we headed back to my condo. Bryleigh had fallen asleep, so Rhys carried her up so he could put her in the bed. I was happy she tired herself out.

As he did that, I went into my bedroom to change out of my clothes. I wanted to take a quick shower before getting into bed. Stripping down, I grabbed my towel and wrapped my body in it, before grabbing my shower caddy. Turning on my heels, I saw Rhys walk into the bedroom and close the door behind himself.

"What are you doing?" I asked as he slowly walked closer to me, sexily chewing on some gum. It was wrong for him to be so fine.

He didn't respond, he just towered over me and removed my towel. Shoving me back onto the bed, he peeled his clothes off, and placed his gum in the trash. Instead of getting up and kicking him out, I laid there paralyzed, watching him unveil his perfectly chiseled body. His toffee complexion was beautiful, and his strong arms, chest, and abs were carved perfectly.

Yanking my ankles to bring me to the edge of the bed, he swiped his dick across my lips, before I opened my mouth to take him in. It's almost like he had me under a spell. Gliding my mouth up and down his dick, I played with his balls while he moaned subtly. I kept getting more and more into it, sucking his dick like I was a porn star. Before I knew it, he was exploding in my mouth. Bending down to wrap his big hand around my neck, he began sucking my lips. He then put me on all fours, before lying under me and bringing my pussy to his mouth.

"Shit, Rhys," I whimpered as I rode his face slowly.

"Don't be shy, Summer," he groaned, pulling my pussy further into his mouth.

I listened and began to grind harder on his face until I released everything inside of me. He slid from under me, and then got behind me, pushing himself inside. I had yet to sleep with Hakim, so I was craving to be fucked.

"Uh," I moaned lightly when he slammed my head into the pillow.

Before I could catch my breath, he was blowing my back out as if he loathed me. My body was reacting before my mind could grasp what was going on, and before I knew it, my inner thighs were drenched.

"Mmmm, uuuh, uuuh, aaah, oh my gosh!" I cried out as he continued to beat my pussy to a pulp. We both yelled out together, as he filled me up with his seeds. As soon as I came that last time, I felt guilty.

"Get out, Rhys."

"What?" he panted.

"You have to go."

I hopped up out of the bed and grabbed my towel from the floor. He got up as well, and just pulled his clothes on. I expected to hear him argue, but he just left. I guess that was what I wanted, right?

Kimberlyn

I was going out to lunch with my grandmother today, and I couldn't wait. I'd been pretty wrapped up in my life with TQ, and the fact that I had class, assignments, and a baby coming didn't help. However, I planned to spend the whole day with her, filling her in on everything.

As I spread lotion all over my legs, TQ walked into the bedroom to watch me. I gave him a shy smile, before turning my attention back to the task at hand. Walking over to me, he got down on his knees, and placed my legs onto his shoulders. Planting kisses up my inner thigh, he grabbed onto the waistline of my underwear to pull them down.

"Tarenz, no, I have to go somewhere," I giggled as I watched my panties go past my ankles.

In typical TQ fashion, he declined to say anything back as he pushed his face into my center, sucking on my clit once he came in contact with it. I threw my head back in ecstasy, and gripped the beautiful white comforter in my hands. I realized that being pregnant made me much more sensitive down there, so it was no surprise that I was releasing only a few moments into the action.

"Mmmm," I caressed the back of his head, which bore a freshly cut fade. "I love you," I whispered as he kept eating like I wasn't even talking.

Lifting one of my legs from his shoulders, he pushed it towards my small belly and really got in there. He kept his mouth latched onto my pussy as if they were one, as his tongue moved widely over my clit. The feeling was unexplainable, and in no time, my pelvis was tightening again. The sound of him moaning lightly as if this was the best meal in the world, only heightened my senses. Whimpering like a little wounded puppy dog, I tried to back away a bit but he gripped my ass cheeks. I was in a state of pure euphoria, and if I were to look into a mirror, my eyes would surely be rolling back.

"Ahh, ahh," my voice trembled as if I were sitting in the middle of a cold blizzard naked. I began winding my hips slowly against his mouth, loving every minute of the head he was giving me. "Baby, uuhh, mm," I bit down on my lip, attempting to stifle the loud ass screams and yowls I wanted to release. Finally, for the third time, I exploded. He stayed down there for a moment, kissing my lower lips sensually and gently while I quivered. My legs were shaking uncontrollably to the point where it was embarrassing.

As he stood to his feet, I stared at him as if he were a mythical creature. And with the way he'd just feverishly ate me out, he *was* a mythical creature. Half smiling, he turned on his heels and went into the bathroom to brush his teeth. My body was still experiencing the orgasm as I laid back letting it all out. I just wanted to ball up into the fetal position.

I never understood when girls would say their man's sex game was too bomb to leave, that was until now. I felt like singing Marvin

Gaye and Tammi Terrell's song "Ain't No Mountain High Enough", because it was so true. I would walk a thousand miles like Vanessa Carlton said, for this nigga and that sex.

"You okay?" he asked after spitting his Listerine out.

"Ye-yeah, I'm okay." I nodded and stood to my feet slowly. This nigga had me light headed, which was not okay since I needed to be somewhere. It was so unfair how he could impair my body like that.

He handed me a warm, soapy towel that I didn't even see him walk in with. I took it with me back to the bathroom, peed, wiped myself with it, and then washed my hands after putting it into the hamper.

"I'm probably not gonna see you until tonight, so I needed my fix," he smirked.

"Ye-yeah, that's fine," I nodded again, still in la land over those three powerful orgasms.

He pulled me into him, and then kissed my lips gently, causing my clit to throb. He then backed away, wearing that sexy ass smile, as his deep blue eyes lit up the room and my fucking life.

"See you later, shorty." And with that he left the bedroom.

I grabbed some new panties from the drawer I kept over here, and then I was out the door as well.

***

I decided to bring my grandmother to Deuxave, a French restaurant on Commonwealth. She loved French food she said, and when I told TQ, he said this place was really good. I tried to convince her to come to his family's restaurant, Verenich, but she said she wanted to go when TQ was available because she didn't trust that I knew what to get. He agreed to take us this coming Wednesday night.

We both chose the three-course meal, which was a whopping $75 per person. My grandma had to take some of her blood pressure medicine after we ordered, which I thought was hilarious. Although a wonderful provider, and willing to buy my cousin and I anything, she was very frugal when it came to herself. But since I was paying, there would be none of that.

"Are you sure, honey? I will pay for half of the bill," she said before sipping her ice water.

"No Ma, I have it, I told you. This is the least I can do for all the stuff you've bought me over the years."

"I know, but that doesn't count, Kimberlyn. I was your provider."

"But you didn't have to be. You're my grandmother, not my mom. You could've abandoned me but you didn't. You could've treated me badly or only given me the bare necessities but you didn't."

"Yes, but you didn't ask to be here, your fast ass mother brought you here," she replied as we both laughed.

It was crazy that my mother Stephanie, when alive, was known in Boston for getting around, yet I was unbelievably opposite from her. She lost her virginity at thirteen years old to a twenty-one-year-old man, and I was a virgin until twenty-one. I guess in some cases the apple does fall very far from the tree.

"Where do you get money, Beri?" my grandmother asked, using my childhood nickname.

"I've designed some people's websites."

"You used to do that before, and you could never afford a $150 dinner bill." She stared into my eyes, waiting for me to tell her what she already knew.

"Tarenz gives me money, weekly."

"Weekly? How much?"

"Only like fifteen." I began munching on the salad the waiter had brought to the table a few moments prior.

"Only like fifteen what?" she raised her brow, holding her fork up.

"Grand, Ma. It's just so I can get around without needing anything, and in case an emergency happens. Like car trouble or something."

"Oh yes, what is that thing you're driving again? A Tesser?" she stabbed her salad.

"A Tesla, Ma," I chuckled at her.

"And you say it charges? Like a phone?"

"Yep."

"Well, honey, it sure is nice. I felt like Michelle Obama riding around in that damn thing, so I can only imagine how you feel driving it. But honey, don't become accustomed to the money he gives you."

"I won't. What God giveth, he can taketh away."

"Exactly!"

"Hello, ladies," the waitress approached the table. "I am going on lunch, so Amikka here will be your waitress."

I smiled but when Amikka and I made eye contact, I realized she was the bitch I punched in the club. I could've sworn she lived in New York because of her accent, but I guess I was wrong. How dare that nigga tell me to come here, somewhere I could possibly be waited on by one of his past hoes?

"Great," my grandmother answered as Amikka and I stared intently into one another's eyes.

"Is there anything I can get you guys?" Amikka asked nicely, sarcasm dripping from her tone.

I wanted a refill, but I didn't want her ass to get it. She may spit in it, and could I blame her? I punched her ass down a flight of stairs in a popular Boston club. It was humiliation at its best.

"No—"

"Oh, she would like a refill on her drink," my grandmother cut me off.

"Be right back!" she pranced off.

We continued eating, and a few moments later, another waiter came to the table with our plates. He placed them down, asked us if we needed anything else, then walked away. I did tell him I wanted a drink, but I was hoping he didn't tell Amikka to get it. She hadn't come back so I was praying that she'd forgotten about it, allowing someone else to get my drink. My dreams were crushed when I saw her switching over to the table with my glass.

"Ah!" I screamed when she spilled the ice-cold ass lemonade all over the bottom half of my dress.

"Oh, I am so sorry!" she fake pouted and grabbed a cloth napkin from another table. She began wiping my bottom half, but slowed down when she felt the hardness of my small belly.

"You stupid bitch!" I growled, still feeling the effects of the cold ass drink.

"Kimberlyn!" my grandmother looked at me like I'd lost my mind.

"I said I was sorry, miss. I can get you another—"

"You did it on purpose, and if I wasn't pregnant, I would whoop your ass, you fucking dummy!"

"Kimberlyn! Can we get the check, please?" my grandmother said, staring at me angrily.

"Sure, and again, I am very sorry."

"Ma, she is one of TQ's little groupies. She did that on purpose. I punched her at a club once, so she's probably getting me back."

"Why didn't you say something in the beginning? We could have told the initial waitress we wanted someone else, Kimberlyn."

"Sorry."

"Don't be sweetie, it's okay," she chuckled.

The manager ended up throwing the bill out altogether, so we didn't pay a thing. My grandma asked for a new waiter, since we decided to stay and finish our meals. The food was really good, and so was the conversation, so my dress being damp didn't bother me too much. After lunch, we went to the mall, and then I took her home. We talked until about ten o'clock at night, and then I drove to TQ's condo.

"How was it?" he asked as soon as I walked in.

He was on the couch looking sexy as fuck in boxers, basketball shorts, and socks. He was shirtless, and his deep caramel complexion was heavenly. I could see the TV in his blue eyes as he stared at me, eating Cheerios like he always did.

"Did you forget that your side chick works for Deuxave?"

He frowned at me like he didn't know what I was saying, but then that beautiful smile appeared again like it always did when he had fucked up.

"Oh shit, I forgot that was where I met her crazy ass. I'm sorry, shorty, and that's not my side chick." He kissed the corner of my mouth.

"Whatever. I'm gonna shower, the bitch spilled my drink on me."

He burst into laughter, but when I turned to look at him he stopped.

"Can I come?" he quizzed.

"No, fuck you."

He laughed again, but soon after, he rushed me from behind, picking me up and carrying me into the bathroom.

Britain

"Fuck did you need? It's late and I have somewhere to be tomorrow," I told Tekeya as I plopped down on the couch.

She was still in the house I bought, and it didn't look like she was planning to leave anytime soon. I know she still had three months, but because I was so anxious to get her up out of here, a nigga was hoping to see a couple of boxes around.

"I didn't tell you to come so damn late. I told you I needed to talk to you earlier in the fucking day, Britain. It's 10pm, and you're just now getting here?" she frowned and sipped some apple juice. Tekeya was a lover of alcohol, and you would never catch her drinking juice or water. *Maybe that's beer*, I wondered.

"Whatever, talk."

"Don't you remember this time last year? How cold it was in Boston, and how we would cuddle up together?"

"No, I don't remember that, Key. All I remember is arguing and fighting with you."

"Well maybe that never happened, but I would have liked for it to happen. You know, when you explained to me that we were never happy, I thought about it a lot after. You were right." She tucked her feet under her butt on the couch. "All we did was bicker with one another, unless we were having sex," she chuckled and gulped some more juice or beer. "What do you think it would have been like if we had have gotten along better?"

"I don't know; I don't really think about it to be honest."

"You don't wonder about how good things would be between us if we tried harder for the relationship? Like, imagine if I hadn't been so caught up in the past, or if you hadn't ever cheated on me."

"You were crazy before I cheated," I replied, and we both chortled lightly.

"Can you blame me? When we were just in the talking stage, there were girls telling me I would never be able to claim you, so I was already on edge."

"Not my fault."

"I know. I should've been more secure." She looked down at the laminate flooring, while tapping her long ass nails on her juice glass. "Can I ask you something?"

"Okay?"

"Why did you cheat on me? Did I do something wrong or—"

"Key, don't—"

"No, I'd like to know. Maybe I can learn for my next man so he can be faithful to me. You know it really broke me down to see you being with other girls."

I looked away from her, before gaining eye contact again.

"I did what I did because I could, and because I felt like I was missing something, even though I had you."

"So I didn't fulfill your needs?"

"Yeah, I guess. Key, what you have to understand is that I wasn't raised to be Heathcliff Huxtable from *The Cosby Show*. From the time I could talk, I was groomed to have multiple women. If it wasn't my father, it was my older brother, TQ. I'd never even seen a man be faithful until my brother Rhys, and even he slipped up once. My father always had other women, and so did his married friends."

"So you're saying it's right?"

"I'm not saying it's right. I'm saying that was all I knew, ma."

"Well if that was how you were raised, how can you say that it was my fault that you weren't faithful? Even if I was fulfilling your needs then, you still would've cheated."

"No, that's not true because—"

"Because you're with that bitch from the park," she stared into my eyes. "Oh, you thought I didn't know? How could I not know when people tell me they've seen you out together? Don't think I don't know some of your associates, Britain."

"Wasn't trying to hide it, I just didn't tell you. I have to go, Key—"

"Wait, before you go, just have dinner with me."

"I really don't—"

"Like a farewell dinner, Britain. This is the end and I think I should get some closure. This isn't fair to me, but if we can just have one more sit down, all will be somewhat well."

"Fine, but it better be ready because like I said, I have somewhere to be tonight and early in the morning."

"Oh it is, come on." She hopped up and grabbed my hand.

Following her into the kitchen, I saw a big glass pan of lasagna with steam still coming from it. She must've just pulled that shit out when I came because it was piping hot. The smell of it was intoxicating, and I suddenly felt a sense of urgency to eat.

I sat down, and watched her pull some plates from the cabinet. She piled some food onto each plate, and then turned to look at me as they sat on the stove.

"Go wash your hands, Britain. It's sad that I still have to tell you that," she smiled.

I sighed as I got up and went into the half bathroom by the kitchen. I quickly scrubbed my hands with the loud ass Bath and Body Works soap, then reentered the kitchen. The plates were sitting on the table, and Tekeya was sitting across from where I was seated prior.

"Oh, would you like something to drink?"

"Water bottle if you have it."

"Okay."

She got up as I sat down, and while she was bent over in the fridge, I switched our plates quietly. I didn't think Tekeya would poison me or some shit, but I was naturally a paranoid person. I guess because of my line of work. I always did this when she cooked, and she never knew. I felt like people took better care of their plate versus others. A meatball will fall on the floor, and they'll drop that shit right on your plate. The only person I trusted wholeheartedly with my food was my mama.

"Here you go," she set my water in front of me, and then set her refilled glass of juice down.

"So have you been looking for a place like I asked?" I stuffed some of the lasagna into my mouth. It was damn near perfect.

"So you still want me to move?"

"Yes I want you to move, Key, fuck is you talking about? How do you think my girl will feel knowing I'm allowing you to stay up in here rent and bill free?"

"It shouldn't matter, I was here first. And you shouldn't allow her to make decisions about your life. You haven't even been with her that long."

"She didn't make the decision, I did. After that calling the police shit, and causing a scene at my place of business, I was done being nice. You need to get on the good foot and find a place quickly."

"Calm down, nigga. If I don't find anything before my three months are up, my brother and his wife will let me come stay with them."

"That's good. I'm glad you have family willing to take you in."

We continued to talk a little, and by the time I was finished with my big ass piece, I was stuffed. It was almost midnight by now, and I knew Goldie would have a lot to say to me. I told her to come to my crib and stay the night with me since I was leaving for Tallahassee tomorrow morning. She'd been there for a cool minute now with no sign of me, so I was sure I would get an earful.

Key stood up to get the plates, and stumbled back a little. I got up in time to catch her, and she giggled while looking up into my eyes.

"You okay?" I asked.

"Ye-yeah, I'm good. I umm, I'm just feeling a bit under the weather," she slurred and smiled.

"Fuck were you drinking?" I picked up the glass and stuck my nose in it. It was definitely apple juice so I was confused.

"Let's go chill, Britain," she rubbed my bicep after throwing the plates into the sink.

"Nah Key, move."

As I lightly fought with her to keep her from rubbing me, it dawned on me what had happened. If I was right, I was gonna be furious.

"You put something in my food, Key?"

"Huh?"

"Did you put some shit into my food? I switched our plates and now you look high as a fucking kite!"

"You—" She looked into the sink at the plates as if she would find some answers. "You switched the plates? Why did you- oh shit!" she slurred, turning her attention back to me and panicking.

"Wow, you are a trip, Key." I folded my arms, leaning up against the sink as she hurled everything from her body into the toilet in the half bathroom. Walking in there, I picked her head up using her hair and said, "Be out of my shit in one week or I'm murking yo' ass. And that's on my fucking mama."

WHAM!

I banged her head into the toilet seat, busting her nose. And with that, I was gone.

Tekeya was a fucking shady hood rat bitch, and there was no being nice to her. I tried, I really did, because I felt she was owed that. But what she did tonight was unacceptable. If she wasn't out of that house one week from today, I was filling her up with slugs.

Matikah

Like every morning for the past two weeks, I was exited to go into work. I loved my job, and I also loved that Isabetta only allowed me to have a small number of clients per day, until I got the hang of things. I mean, I was good at what I did, but I was still a little scared to be working on real customers, and not having my teacher there to back me up if something went wrong. Isabetta was a big help, but I needed to remember that she was my boss and not my instructor. She was paying me to perform, not paying me to teach me.

When I entered the spa, I grabbed a time-off sheet before taking it to my room to fill it out. Lendsey told me his family, which meant his actual family and a whole bunch of niggas, were throwing a costume party. I didn't want to miss that at all, so I thought I'd request it some time ahead to be sure it was granted.

Once I was done filling the form out, I walked it to Isabetta's office. Knocking on the door, I looked over my shoulder to be sure no one was creeping into my room. Isabetta said it was safe to leave our belongings inside our rooms, but I didn't trust these girls; especially because I had some expensive shit that I'd seen them eye on multiple occasions.

"Come in," Isabetta called out.

I entered, but was surprised to see her teary eyed, sitting behind her desk. She quickly grabbed a handful of tissues, and wiped her eyes before looking back up at me.

"I can come back la—"

"No, no it's fine. Work comes first. Sit down, please," she smiled; well, she gave a forced one that is.

"I just came to drop off this time-off request. I know I just got here, but it's for an important event. I heard it was busy around that time, so I wanted to make arrangements as early as possible."

"I appreciate that." She reached her hand out to take the paper.

"If you don't mind me asking, what's wrong?"

"Umm," she sniffled and looked off. "My sister, the one who came in here going crazy on your first day. She'd been missing since last week, but they found her body this morning. Someone broke into her apartment and killed her. She was lying in the bed, dead, with flies everywhere," she sobbed.

I thought I was gonna pass out when she said Dania was her sister. I knew exactly who killed her, and I really didn't know what to say. I was all for Lendsey having that hoe knocked off, but seeing Isabetta crying her eyes out had me feeling differently.

"I-I'm sorry to hear that. I don't know what to say, maybe you should go home."

"I have a business to run, Matikah. That's the only downside to being the boss, you don't get time off to grieve and things like that."

"But you should. I don't mind losing a day's pay if you need to close the spa." It was the least that I could do.

"You're sweet, Matikah, but no. Go ahead and start your shift. I appreciate your listening ear." She stood up, smoothing down her business skirt in the process.

"Okay, let me know if you change your mind," I turned to leave.

"I won't. I just hope they find the muthafucker who did it and run their ass up a flagpole."

My back was still turned, but I was standing there, not moving. I chose not to respond, and just left out, closing the door behind me.

As I walked slowly to the front with my head down, I bumped into someone. When I picked my head up, I saw it was that chick, Isyss. She had a purple bob today, and lipstick to match. She reminded me of the rapper Charli Baltimore for some reason. She didn't look like her, but she had light skin and colored hair.

"Excuse me," I walked around her. When I got to the front, I noticed she was behind me, just standing there. "Did you have a question?"

"Yeah, what happened to Isabetta's sister?"

"Someone killed her." I looked over my shoulder.

"Do you know who it was?"

"How the hell would I know who it was?" By this time, I'd turned my body to face her completely.

"Let's just say I was in the club that night, and I saw her tell the bouncer to ask some guy in the VIP something. He was the same guy whose lap you were dancing in."

"What's your point?"

"My point is that I think whomever she was sending messages to, had something to do with it. And if he did, that means you know about it because you're clearly fucking him."

"I'm sorry, I'm missing the part where her talking to my man, connects him to her murder. The two don't go hand in hand, unfortunately."

"They do to me."

"If you had dreams of being in law, stick to working at the spa, boo, because you'd lose every case."

"I wonder what Isabetta would think if I told her about the little incident at the club," she moved closer to me.

"She won't think anything of it. I'm sure she knows how thirsty her sister was over him. She had his name tatted, for God's sake."

"Maybe I should find out, have her look into him."

"Do what you gotta do, Isyss. I just hope you don't end up like Dania, trying to play Inspector Gadget." I shoulder bumped her and walked to my room to prepare for my first waxing appointment.

That bitch had me fucked up. I didn't know what her beef was with me, but she needed to back the fuck off before I whooped her ass, or worse, got Lendsey on that bitch.

A little over seven hours later I was done, and my feet were killing me. It felt good though. It made me happy that I'd been working hard all day on something that I loved. I wasn't anxious to hurry up and go home during the day, at all. I guess it's true when they say if you love what you do, you'll never work a day in your life.

As I was leaving, Isyss and I made eye contact. I winked at her ghetto ass, and continued to sashay out with my Birkin on my arm. Getting into my car, I cut the heat on, and peeled out of that parking lot. I'd initially planned to tell Lendsey what had happened, but I wanted to give her a chance. I knew if I said anything, he would off her immediately.

CHAPTER EIGHT

One month later…

“I have to go,” Indiya chuckled as I lied between her legs, kissing her neck.

“Don’t go this time,” I said, as trailed my lips down her collarbone, before taking her nipple into my mouth.

I’d been chilling with and fucking her on a daily almost. I never planned to become cool with her, but the shit just happened. I enjoyed her company, and the fact that she didn’t press me about what we were to each other. She knew all about my situation with Summer, not too many details, and she only listened and gave me advice when she felt I needed it. She wasn’t an escort with me. I mean, she was, but I wouldn’t even remember until she mentioned having to go to work. Best of all though, she kept my mind off of my ex.

“I didn’t go yesterday, and your mom is gonna kill me if I pull the same thing,” she chuckled.

"I got you, and I will even tell her for you." I placed my chin against her flat stomach so I could look into her face, as she rubbed my baldhead.

"I need the money though, Rhys. I've been missing multiple days a week since I met you."

"You wanna go?"

"For the money."

"Is that the only reason why?"

"Of course it is. I would much rather spend time with you, or make my money other ways. I don't have that luxury just yet."

I kissed back up her body slowly until I reached her lips. Feeling between her legs, I toyed with her clit until she got wet as hell. Once she did, I grabbed a condom from the nightstand, opened it, and slid it down. I had a couple boxes all over the nightstand, waiting to be used. I was fucking shorty that much.

"Mmm," she cooed once I got inside of her.

Like always, she was warm, wet, and tight. I maneuvered my tongue into her mouth as I moved in and out of her gently. Pinning her hands behind her head, I wound my hips into her, slamming in and pulling out slowly. Seeing her perfectly round and perky breasts moving every time I thrust into her, had me about to nut.

Excluding my baby mama, Indiya was the sexiest bitch I'd ever come in contact with. Not to mention she had a dope ass personality, and the pussy was fire.

"Shit," I grumbled, enjoying the feeling of her soft thighs wrapped around my waist. "Tell me you're gonna stay."

"I ca—"

I sped up, killing her shit so that she wouldn't say what I didn't want to hear. I drilled into her with force, and I knew soon enough I would be releasing. She exploded, but I kept up my pace.

"Tell me," I pinned her hands down harder as I plowed into her sopping wet center.

"I-I'm gonna stay!"

"Fuck!" I growled as I filled the condom up. Dropping down onto her, I let her hands go and kissed her soft lips.

"Eto bylo zdorovo, (That was great)," she panted.

I pecked her once more before rolling off of her and lighting a blunt. After taking a couple pulls, I passed it to her, and we continued to smoke on the blunt in silence for a bit.

"Do you want me to quit?"

"I don't know. I just don't like what you do I guess. I mean, I didn't care before, but now I do for some reason."

"I see."

"What happens when you work?"

"Huh?"

"Tell me how it goes."

"Well, I meet them at a restaurant, usually. We have dinner, while I ask them questions about themselves. They're usually always rich older men with wives and kids at home. And they always have the same story: their wives are too boring or nag too much, but that they love them. Then they ask about me, and I give them the made up background of Tess Fredricks, my fake name. After dinner, we go to a suite booked by your mother or sister, and that's where it goes down. The thing I love about your mother and sister is that they make every guy take an STD and HIV test prior to the date."

"Good practices. And you've never came while working?"

"No, I haven't. By the time it starts feeling good, they're already climaxing. Some guys just want to stare at me and jack off."

"Damn, you don't give blow jobs, you don't let them hit raw, yet they still request you."

"I'm surprised myself. I feel like I'm no fun. But then again, most of them just want conversation with a pretty woman. Me sleeping with them is a bonus so they don't ask for much. The younger guys are different, well they pretend to be, but they nut just as early." She passed the blunt back.

"I've thought about eating your pussy but I don't know," I spoke honestly. She sat up and then got off the bed to grab her undergarments and dress. "Where are you going?"

"I'm going to work."

"What? You just said you wouldn't go."

"I said I wouldn't go because I thought I was gonna be chilling with a nigga who didn't see me as a whore."

"What? I don't—"

"Then why make comments like that? You thought about giving

me head, but you don't know. If I wanna feel like a hoe, I will get paid for it at least." She pulled her thong up her perfect frame.

"Indiya, relax." I got off the bed, and picked her up. She wrapped her legs around my waist, as I hugged her small torso and kissed her collarbone. "I didn't mean it like that, but then again, what other way could you have taken it. I promise when we're together I don't think of you as a hoe. I just spoke my mind, and I shouldn't have said that. If I thought you were nasty or something, I wouldn't fuck you at all, condom or not."

She just tousled her brown hair as I carried her back to the bed. Lying her down, I tugged her lace panties off, and spread her legs. Her pussy was beautiful, and perfectly shaven. I kissed her inner thighs, while looking up into her eyes, and then took her clit into my mouth. She tasted just as good as she looked. I reached up to play with her nipples as I sucked her button like a jolly rancher candy. I switched back and forth between sucking hard and then softly, and when she released, I lapped it all up. I hadn't gotten enough though, especially listening to her sweet moans, so I kept going in.

"Rhys, oh, oh my gosh," she cried out as I gave her the best tongue beat down I could ever give.

Again, she released, but I didn't let up until she had her fourth orgasm. I then just planted a few kisses, before trailing them up her stomach.

"I'm gonna talk to my mom about getting you another job within the family."

"Okay," she nodded and panted heavily.

I was definitely feeling Indiya Nikolaev… Maybe Summer was right; it was best we be apart.

I said a prayer before getting out of the car and entering my parents' house. I wanted to stay calm and keep this meeting civilized for as long as possible, but you never knew when you put my dad and I in a room. My father had a way of pissing me off like no one else could, and if he thought he was gonna talk shit like he did the last time I saw him, he was out of his monkey ass mind.

I was his son, but I was still a grown ass man and nobody was gonna disrespect me. I didn't give a fuck what they were the boss of, or what they ran, if you didn't come correct out of your mouth when talking to Tarenz Quinton, you were bound to get your face blown off. I didn't play them grown ass man disrespecting me games. Matter fact, I didn't play when anyone tried do that shit. Every man, woman, and child better recognize and shape the fuck up when I enter into a room, period point blank.

"What's good?" I walked into his office. Instead of sitting in the chair across from his huge wooden desk, I sat down on the plush ass couch like I was there to kick it. Fuck homie, he had to regain my respect if he wanted it.

"Is that how we're gonna start this meeting?" he asked, standing over me with his hands in his pockets. I just looked up at his ass, waiting for him to fucking get to business. "I see we're being childish today. Tarenz, I need to know what your plans are in making Gang whole." He sat on the La-Z-Boy adjacent to me.

"Fuck is you talking about?"

"Like we discussed last time—"

"Nah, we didn't discuss shit last time! I came up in here and you got to popping off at the mouth like I'm some little ass boy or some shit! That's what the fuck happened last time. Now again, what the fuck are you talking about?"

He stared at me, wearing a smile to hide his anger. I knew he was itching to pounce over on me and choke me until I died. I didn't give a fuck though, because like I'd told his ass before, I'm not that same teenager who cowered every time his father got loud with him. My brothers and I had grown up and no longer damn near pissed our pants when we thought our father was angry. I didn't give a fuck. He could eat the shit out of my ass with a spoon for all I cared.

"Tarenz, you killed Gang's right-hand man. You murdered someone that aided him in making all of that good money we like."

"Go on."

"We need to make things better because right now, Gang is not too happy about working with us. And can you really blame him? I mean, first you take his bitch—"

"Watch your mouth old man."

"You took his girl, and then murdered the person he worked with and called his best friend."

"So what? That's the muthafuckin' game and you know it! Niggas die all the damn time in this shit, and sometimes it's the people closest to us. Think about Uncle Boris!"

My uncle Boris was my dad's younger brother who was killed here in Boston. When he and my dad came over from Russia, they started working with this big time Russian mafia boss, Ermolai "Emilio" Petrov. They were basically his muscle and messenger boys aka nobodies. Anyhow, only six months into working for him, my uncle was killed while transporting some money for his ass, but Emilio just shrugged the shit off. My father was so enraged that he spent months gaining muscle and making a name for himself, right under Emilio's nose. About a year and a half later, Emilio was killed and my father became who he is today.

"Yes, people die all the time, Tarenz, but you don't continue to do business with the people who have killed your people! You are making this very hard for me! Why did you even do it?!" He stood up.

"Because he put his hands on a friend of mine."

"He put his hands on a friend of yours," he repeated after me as he paced the same area with his hands in his pockets. "A fucking friend? Ty durak! (You're a fool!). So what! This is a crime family, not a battered women's shelter!"

I admit I probably shouldn't have killed Peel, but seeing Hayden's face like that pissed me off. I hated men who put their hands on women, but I especially hated the ones who fought women like they were niggas. Slapping her a time or two is unacceptable, but to box her ass like she was equal to you was fucked up.

Many times when I was around eight and nine, my father would take Rhys and I to his friends' homes. One in particular, this guy named Grisha, would punch his wife and just whoop her ass. You could hear her screaming and crying from the room they were in, and my father and his friends would just play cards, smoke, drink, and talk like nothing was happening. Not one of them would get up and stop him. That shit was traumatizing as fuck, so one day I opened my young eight-year-old mouth in her defense. All my dad did was snatch me up by my collar, slam me into a wall, and curse me out in Russian for being disrespectful to Grisha. He did all of that in front of his friends because I asked if I could go check on her. As I got older, I developed a hatred for women beaters.

"Nothing to say, huh?" he quizzed.

"Nothing to be said. I killed him and he's not coming back. I don't care to make Gang whole, and neither should you. Quit kissing his ass and get to work on finding someone else who can make money in Boston."

"You know, Tarenz, if I ever get killed, I beg that you don't become the head of this shit. Crime families aren't meant to be run by little ass bitches who kill when they get in their feelings. You have a girl, and that's the only one you need to be protecting."

"I protect who the fuck I want to protect! I ain't gon' sit by like some bitch ass nigga and watch a man put his hands on a woman! I'm not like you! And the only thing you need to be worried about when it comes to getting killed is hoping it ain't me who murders you."

"Tarenz! I will murder you!" he hollered after me as I left his office and then the house.

Once I got in the car, I punched the fuck out of my wheel. I was tired. I was tired of dealing with this nigga and him trying to please Gang. Gang worked for *us*, yet he was running around giving ultimatums like he ran shit. He may run that old geezer up in there, but he don't run me at all. If he's gonna cry and moan about his homie getting killed, he needs to get the fuck outta the game. If he were a real nigga, he would enact revenge on the muthafucka who did it. I hoped he did too.

On my way out of the driveway, I had my car phone pull up Jayce. Me and this nigga needed to have a talk ASAP.

"What's up, player?" he answered, sounding high as a giraffe's pussy.

"Meet me at the warehouse."

"Shit, umm, TQ, I'm kind of busy right no—"

"Be at the muthafuckin' warehouse in twenty minutes or the fishermen will be pulling your body up in their nets with all the other sea creatures," I hung up.

When I got to the warehouse, I saw him leaning up against the hood of his car, smoking a blunt. He had the nerve to smile and put his hand out to dap me up like everything was gravy.

"Come on," I waved him as I walked in.

"TQ, ma-man, where are we going?" he hesitated.

"I wanna talk."

We finally walked into the warehouse, and into a smaller room that was like a beat down office. I closed the door behind him, and then went to sit behind the desk. He took a seat in the chair across from me, and stared at me with a fearful expression. Why was he so on edge?

"You've been drinking?" I asked.

"Nah, well, I had a couple glasses of bourbon, but that was like six hours ago. It's what, 7pm now? So yeah, like six hours ago."

I just stared at him in silence, and then reached into my pocket for some gum. I didn't take my eyes off of him while doing so. Something was weird about him. I wanted to chalk it up to him being drunk and high, but my mind wouldn't let me.

After chewing for a couple of moments, I placed my forearms on the desk and clasped my hands together.

"Jayce, I don't know what the fuck is going on with you, but you need to get with the damn program. If you miss one more party, meeting, anything that is thrown by QCF, I will end you. You won't even know it's coming either. You're acting shady as fuck, and before I feel like you can do anything to me or my family, I will have something done to you. Vy ponimayete? (You understand?)"

"Umm, I—"

"Vy ponimayete!"

"I don't speak Russian, TQ, you know that," his voice trembled slightly.

"Otvet' mne. (Answer me.)" I walked around and placed my .45 to his head.

"TQ, come on man, please. Yo-you know I don't—"

I burst into laughter, cutting him off mid sentence.

"Glupyy. (Stupid.)" I put my gun away, chuckling. "Come on." I gripped his shoulder so that he'd get up. We left the warehouse together, but before we went our separate directions to get into our cars, I grabbed his shoulder and said, "I hope we have a newfound understanding."

"Of course."

"Khorosho. (Good)."

Goldie

Britain's real estate agent finally found a condo that I loved in Downtown Boston, less than ten minutes away from him. All the places we looked at were no more than fifteen minutes from his place on Washington Street, which I'm sure was on purpose. Anyway, I would start moving next week, and boy I couldn't wait. I couldn't get out of hood ass Mattapan fast enough.

KNOCK! KNOCK!

As I was taping up one of the boxes of summer clothes, I heard a knock at my door. It was strange because since I lived in an apartment, you rarely got knocks. Usually, someone would call to be buzzed in. Not sure what to do, I opted out of asking who it was, and just slowly looked through the peephole. My face immediately transformed into a frown when I saw my sister standing there with a plate.

"Is mom dead?" I opened the door.

"What?" she giggled. "No, why would you think that?"

"Because you're at my residence. We don't speak, so the only reason I could think of was a death in the family."

"Well, the good Lord has blessed mama to see another day," she grinned, and tried to walk around me into my apartment, but I blocked her.

"I see you're still putting on that church act."

"Not an act, I'm devoted to God. And maybe if you had have been as loyal to the Man above as I am, mama wouldn't despise you so."

"Chenaye, what the fuck do you want?"

"Can I come in first?"

"You can, but make it quick because I have some company coming over in a little bit and I don't want you here."

"Who is it? Britain Quinton?"

"No, it's not," I responded, a little taken aback that she knew who I was dating. I closed the door and sat down on the couch.

"Well, I don't mean to be here long, I just wanted to talk to you about some things. Oh, and I brought some cinnamon sugar cookies," she smiled, before setting them on one of the brown boxes nearby.

"Talk to me about what, Naye?"

"I need your help with something. You see, I was dating this guy for a little bit, but for some reason he decided to stop talking to me."

"For some reason?" I raised a brow.

"Yes, I know I did nothing wrong because I mean, I'm me."

"Maybe your pussy was trash."

"Now everyone knows I'm a virgin, Goldie."

"Everyone like who?"

"Long as King Jesus knows, that's all I care about," she smiled. "But like I said, I need your help—"

"Excuse me, how can you come over here and ask me for help like we're close or something, Chenaye? And not only that, how the fuck am I supposed to help you get him back?"

"I know we haven't been close over the years, Goldie. But I prayed about it and God told me he wanted me to mend our precious and fragile relationship."

"Oh my gosh!" I laughed before covering my face with my hands.

"I'm serious, sister. And whatever the Lord tells me to do, is exactly what I do."

"Then why aren't you a virgin?" I smirked.

"Why do you keep saying that? Whatever would make you think I wasn't?"

"You aren't."

"That's not the point here. The point is that you're dating Britain, and I need you to help me get his brother back."

"His brother? Which—"

KNOCK! KNOCK!

What was up with people getting into my building without having to be buzzed up? I bet some nigga broke the lock on the gate again.

"Oh, hey guys," I opened the door for Summer, Matikah, and Kimberlyn. Matikah and Kimberlyn knew of Chenaye, but they'd never met her. I'd wanted to keep it that way, but I guess I could only do so for so long.

I hugged each of the girls when they walked in, and as soon as Summer and Chenaye made eye contact, they began fighting in the middle of the living room. So much for her only doing what the good

Lord tells her.

"Oh my gosh!" Matikah yelled as they screamed, growled, swung, and pulled on one another's hair like they were trying to rip it from the scalp.

"Kimberlyn, get back!" I shouted, not wanting her to get bumped or knocked over. Her stomach wasn't big at all yet, but still.

She slowly did as I asked, and Matikah and I began pulling the girls apart. Once we did, I held onto my sister a little longer to make sure she wouldn't charge Summer again. Chenaye's hair was all over her damn head, and her nose was bleeding. Summer had a cut on her bottom lip, but her dreads were in tact. I guess you couldn't really mess those up.

"Why is she here!" Summer hollered.

"Me? This is *my* sister's home, why are *you* here?!" Chenaye seethed.

"How do you know one another?" Kimberlyn asked, reentering the area.

"This bitch was fucking Rhys while I was with him!" Summer answered.

"I wasn't fucking him, I was trying to! And I would have been successful had you not fucked it all up!"

Summer's frown suddenly softened as she panted, while staring at Chenaye. I was still in disbelief about the fact that Chenaye's fake ass even knew Rhys. It's not like you could run into him in Target, and Chenaye didn't go too many places outside of church, so I had plenty of questions. Then again, she was a fraud so I'm sure she did go other places outside of church, it was just unbeknownst to us all.

"You didn't fuck him?" Summer questioned after a few moments of silence.

"No, we just spent time together. We were getting close, and then all of a sudden he tells me he wants to cut me off," Chenaye grunted, while fixing her shirt sleeves since I'd finally let her go.

"Wait, is this the girl from the picture?" Matikah pointed to Chenaye, and Summer nodded with her eyes closed before sitting down. "So, you kind of broke up with Rhys for nothing?"

"No, no I didn't. Chilling with her wasn't cool either, but fuck. An-and don't forget about Lisa shooting me!"

"What picture?" Chenaye frowned.

"You need to go." I got up and pulled her to the front door, opened it, and shoved her lightly across the threshold.

"Think about what I said Gold—"

BAM! I slammed the door in her face, before sitting back down next to Summer.

"Well, what are you gonna do?" Kimberlyn asked, removing her sandals.

"I'm not even sure. I have a boyfriend now, and I said some things to Rhys that were damn near unforgivable."

"He loves you though, Summer. Lendsey told me how crazy he was about you, so I think he would be happy if you wanted to work on things," Matikah smiled.

"And what about Hakim?"

"Let him down easy," I shrugged and grabbed one of the cookies Chenaye left. I was surprised that she remembered these were my favorite.

"No, no. Regardless of the situation in particular, Hakim is the better man. The picture with Chenaye was just the last straw. Rhys and I weren't good together before that. I can't go back. I have to keep looking forward, and stick by Hakim."

"I don't mean to be callous, but I'm eating for two and I wanna start this big dinner we were so called gonna cook. We can resume the conversation once we're done," Kimberlyn chimed in, making us all laugh.

There was never a dull moment with this crew…

Lendsey

"I cannot work for her any longer," one of the women I was helping find employment sighed.

As I stated before, I helped out with my dad's unemployment agency. We mainly assisted Russian, Slavic, Ukranian, and sometimes Polish people, but every now and then we assisted Americans and other types of foreigners with finding jobs. The reason my dad opened this place was because foreigners have a hard time finding work and employers that will hire them without the right paperwork. I would get them forged paperwork, making them hirable, then find them a job. All of the employers we worked with were aware of the fact that they were hiring immigrants with illegitimate paperwork. Sometimes our people would go out and find jobs with people we weren't affiliated with though. I didn't really like that because they were using my fake paperwork to do so, but whatever.

"What is the problem, Dominika?"

"She is too, she is too, how do you say umm, vlastnyy (bossy; overbearing)?"

"She's mean," I sighed and she nodded. "I can find you something else, but it may take me a couple of days. Did you inform Ms. Hoblan that you'd be looking elsewhere for employment? You know it's important for us to give them notice."

"Yes, I try to explain but my English isn't very good, lyublyu (love)."

"Okay, well you need to practice more, da (yes)?"

"Da. I mean yes, Mr. Quinton."

Dominika was nineteen years old but supporting her three little brothers and sick mother. Her father, Dima, moved the family to America to work under my father, but was killed soon after. That's how it was though working within a crime family. One minute you're breathing and living life, the next you're getting your head blown off at a card game. Because he was a good friend of my father's though, we made sure to help their family out as much as possible. But because Dominika's mother was ill, and her siblings were under the age of eighteen, she had to be the breadwinner.

"Okay, good. English can be easy if you work at it. Now I will call Ms. Hoblan and let her know for you, but if she needs you until we find your replacement, you must help her, okay?"

"Okay," she sighed.

"Here's a check for $3,000 until we find you work. Only start to use it when I clear you from Ms. Hoblan, alright?" I asked as I filled the check out.

She nodded before standing up.

Once she walked out of the glass office I worked in, I picked the phone up to call Ms. Hoblan. Before I could finish dialing, the office assistant, Alyona, walked in.

"Yes?" I frowned, hanging the phone up.

"Mr. Quinton, it's someone here to see you," she fidgeted. I swear this girl always got nervous around me for some reason. We'd been working together for almost a year now, and she still couldn't look me in the eyes. And when we did make eye contact, she would blush or quickly look away. Russian women could be meek sometimes, but it was very rare.

"Who is it?"

"A lady, she says her name is Isabetta Melchior."

Shaking my head at the fact that Dania's sister was here to see me, I then looked to Alyona to let her know she could send her back here.

While I waited, I got up to make myself a drink. By the time I took the first sip of the Brandy, Isabetta was walking into my office. For some weird ass reason, it was just now hitting me that she owned the spa Matikah worked at. I knew I'd heard the name Isabetta before, but I think not hearing her last name attached threw me off. I wonder if Matikah knew.

"Please, have a seat. Would you like something to drink?" I offered.

"Please, I've been liking my drinks strong these days."

I poured her some brandy into a glass, and then walked it over to her. I then sat behind my desk, and stared at her sad ass face for a few.

"So what brings you here?" I quizzed.

"I sent you a notice to come to the funeral. You didn't come though."

"I didn't think it was a good idea for me to show up. I'm not good with funerals anyway. I'm sure the service was beautiful however."

"Yes, it was." She gulped her brandy down. I refilled her glass using my glass decanter, then stuck the top back in. "Thank you. I was wondering if you could maybe help me. Dania let me know that you were someone in Boston, meaning you had connections of all kinds. She wasn't exactly sure how, but she said this was true. No one knows what happened to my sister. I mean, she was shot, but no one knows who did it. There isn't any evidence. I'm wondering, Mr. Quinton, if you can use the connections you have to help my family and me?"

I had to pause for a moment because I didn't know what to say. She was asking the person who ordered her sister's death, to help find the person who did it. If I said no, she may get suspicious. If I said yes, I would have to deliver.

"Isabetta, for some reason, people are under the impression that I'm a well connected individual. That's not exactly the case though. I don't know enough people, nor do I have enough clout to assist you in fingering someone in a murder case," I lied.

"But she said—"

"I know what she said, and I'm sure she believed that. A lot of people believe that to be the case because of my father. He's a very successful businessman, so people think that we run Boston or something."

"I understand. Well, if you come across a way that you can help me, please let me know. Here is my card, my office and cell are on it." She stood up. "Thank you for taking the time to talk with me."

"Anytime." I escorted her out, and then went to tend to my business until it was time for me to go.

I had a gut feeling that Isabetta was not gonna let her sister's murder go unsolved, and I couldn't blame her. It would be wrong for me to have her murdered as well, and it would also draw more attention to the case. Unfortunately, I would just have to sit back and let it ride out. They would never find out who did it, and that was my intention from the get go.

CHAPTER NINE

Summer

A few weeks later…

Ever since I found out that Chenaye didn't actually sleep with Rhys, I couldn't get him off of my mind. I could barely get through the night without waking up, wondering what he was doing. There was no doubt in my mind that I loved him, but the thing keeping me from calling was the fact that he'd spent time with this girl. Cheating physically was bad on it's own, but to cheat emotionally hurt me worse, oddly. It was crazy that me being shot over him didn't bother me as much as I let on. I only brought it up when I felt like I didn't have sound reason to be broken up with him.

I closed my eyes and took a deep breath as I sat in my car across from Rhys' condo. I'd just taken Bryleigh to my mother's earlier than usual, so that I could have some time to stop by his home and talk to him. I wasn't even sure why I wanted to talk, or what I wanted to talk about. I guess I wanted to finally give him the chance to explain himself. I was adamant about sticking by Hakim, so my goal in coming here was not to reunite.

I finally got out of the car, and jogged across the street to his building. I still had my key, so I just walked inside and got on the elevator. Arriving to our floor, I took a few moments for myself, before getting off and walking to his unit. Knocking on the door, I waited and waited for him to answer. He didn't come, so I knocked again. Finally, I heard the locks being twisted, and the door finally came open.

There he stood looking just as sexy as the day is long. His deep blue eyes were sparkling and vibrant, just like his deep caramel complexion. He was shirtless, wearing some boxers, red basketball shorts, and socks, while brushing his perfect teeth. I watched as his bushy eyebrows furrowed upon seeing me, and then I silently asked if I could come in. He sighed lightly before stepping back to let me inside.

When I walked in, I was surprised to see the place was clean and smelling of lavender. Rhys was never home so he never really cleaned, nor did he really make a mess. Still, the place didn't even have his usual cereal bowl lying around, which was surprising. His cereal bowls would stay on the coffee table for months if I didn't clean it. Not only that, but smelling air freshener mixed with his Versace cologne was odd as well. He hated when I tried to spray anything because he "didn't want the place smelling womanly" he said.

I took a seat on the couch once he walked to the back to spit, floss, and rinse. He closed the bathroom door when he went in, which I also found to be out of the ordinary. He finally emerged from the bathroom, and my heart skipped one thousand beats when the sound of female laughter was heard coming from inside. That perfect smile of his was covering his face as he closed the door back, turning his attention to me. I suddenly felt nervous, upset, and sad knowing a woman was here. He brought a woman to the condo we once shared.

"I wasn't expecting you, Summer, is something wrong?" he sat down next to me. I got another whiff of his cologne as I looked into his handsome mug.

"Who's in the bathroom?"

He squinted his eyes as if he didn't understand why I was interrogating him. I knew Rhys like the back of my hand, which means I knew he was gonna skip over my question and ask me one of his own.

"Why are you questioning me about who's in my condo?"

"Never mind. I met Chenaye the other day, and we got into a fight."

"That explains that little cut. Where did you meet her?" he asked nonchalantly as if I didn't just tell him I ran into the reason we broke up.

"I was over Goldie's house, and she was—"

"Goldie is her sister!" he said as if he had the answer to a question on *Who Wants to be a Millionaire?*

"How did you know? I mean, you were dating her so of course you knew."

"I saw a picture of her and Goldie when they were kids while I was at her home. It used to bug the fuck out of me because I couldn't put the face to a name, but now I know. I'm sorry Summer, I don't mean to rush you, but I have things to do today so I'd appreciate it if you got to the point, shorty."

"She told me that you guys never slept together, and I was surprised to hear that. And so, umm, now that I know you've never slept with her, I wa-want to give you a chance to explain."

"I don't care to explain anymore."

"What?"

"I have no interest in explaining anymore. I tried for months to explain to you what the deal was and you didn't care. So now that some bitch you don't know from Adam has said her piece, you wanna give me a chance to explain? Nah."

"I deserve an explanation! You—"

"Oh shit," the girl said, coming out of the bathroom butt ass naked. Her body was banging, and she was really beautiful, which only angered me further.

"Baby, this is my child's mother Summer, and Summer, this is Indiya."

"Nice to meet you," she smiled, quickly snatching a towel from the linen cabinet across from her.

"Likewise," I stated dryly. She just looked from me to Rhys a couple times before going into the bedroom he and I used to share. "Baby?"

"Yeah."

"Already, huh?"

"Are we forgetting about Hakim?"

"I was talking to Hakim way before—" I stopped when I realized what I was saying.

"Way before we broke up, huh?" he chuckled, angrily. "Look, I don't want to explain myself to you, so is there anything else we need to discuss?"

"You hung out with that girl! That is cheating! Going over to her house and spending time with her when you should've been here with Bryleigh and me! Does that new bitch back there know I was shot over you?"

"I admit it was fucked up to be over her house and shit, Summer, I do! But can you blame me? Every time I stepped foot in this muthafucka, you were ready to bite my head off, and over nothing! Accusing me of cheating when I wasn't! So forgive me if I found a friend somewhere!"

"You were cheating, so don't go there."

"Okay," he shrugged.

"Okay?"

"I'm tired of trying to convince you, Summer. You're gonna believe what you want, and frankly, I don't give a fuck anymore."

"Oh, now what, all you care about is, Indiya?"

"I care about her, my child, my job, and even you. What I don't care about is the relationship we once had."

"Fuck you, Rhys! And you better not bring that bitch around my daughter! You will not see Bryleigh if she is here!" I shouted as I shot up off the couch and stormed to the door.

"You're too pretty to be so angry, baby," he called after me as I snatched the door open and left.

I wasn't even in my car good before I broke down. I was used to him coddling me, and telling me how much he loved me. I wanted him to tell me that he loved me more than anything, and that he would never hurt me. That's what he always said when I got mad like that. Hearing him say he didn't care about this, and he didn't care about that, hurt like fuck. I wanted him to care! He had to care! I hated seeing him so calm and relaxed as if his life was peaches and cream. For the first time in a long time I wanted him to get angry like he used to. It seemed like that girl was changing him into the serene faithful man that I always wanted, and that infuriated me. I should've been the one, not her!

I got myself together, then sped off to work. When I got there, I saw Hakim putting his stuff up in the cubby. As I walked by him, I pulled his hand with me and into the back room. Locking the door behind us, I shoved him into the wall and kissed him hungrily. I wanted him to be enough for me to forget about Rhys, and maybe that hadn't happened yet because we hadn't fucked.

"Wait, Summer, stop," he moved my hands from his belt buckle.

"What? Come on."

"No, what the hell is wrong with you? We've never had sex and you want this to be the first time?" he waved around the dusty stock room. "And Paul would murder us both."

I stepped back from him, embarrassed as fuck. I let Rhys get me in my feelings, and now I was acting like some hoe at my place of work. Plopping down on a rickety chair in the room, I dropped my face into my hands.

"Summer, relax. What's wrong?" he kneeled down and rubbed my back.

"I'm sorry, Hakim. I just, I don't know what was going on in my head."

"It's okay. We can pretend this never happened," he snickered and so did I. "Look, I'm gonna take you on a romantic ass date, and after the dessert, we can do it the right way, aight? You deserve more than that."

See, Hakim was a much better man than Rhys. Rhys took my virginity in the back seat of his car. Yes, he had a house full of siblings plus his parents, so we couldn't go there. And yes, he was only seventeen and I fourteen, but still he could've done better. Or maybe I was lying to myself to feel better… Either way, Hakim was the way to go.

Kimberlyn

Today I was gonna be on some top secret shit. I didn't want anyone knowing my plans in fear of them fucking something up. I'd been wanting to do this for weeks now, but because I didn't have the resources I needed at the time, I put it off. But now that I had all the information required, it was game time.

Rushing out of class, I repeatedly checked my watch to make sure that I was on schedule. Because I knew I would be booking it out of the room, I placed my phone deep into my purse to make sure it didn't fall. I made it to my car, and threw all my belongings into the passenger seat, before sliding into the driver's side, cranking up, and peeling out. It was around 3:30pm by the time I got to my destination, so I was right on time. I found a park, and waited about ten minutes, before that bitch, Hayden, pulled up to her apartment building.

I'd been trying to find out where she worked or lived for the longest, but there was no way for me to. I wasn't in contact with anyone who talked to her because Gang was off limits, and Peel, well, I never really talked to him in the first place, but he was dead. That was part of the reason I was here. Anyway, God must've been looking out for me, because while TQ was in the shower, that bitch texted him. He had a code on his phone, but I was on my nigga like white on rice. I paid close attention one day as he typed it in while talking to me.

So when she texted him, I swiftly unlocked his iPhone and read it. She was asking him to come over and talk, and accidentally sent her location as well. I loved that new iPhone feature. I clicked the location and memorized the vicinity. For the past week I've been dropping by, and I finally saw her car parked in front of the building I was currently outside of. Tarenz Quinton was *my* nigga, and I didn't appreciate her reaching out to him for anything, so hell yeah I turned into an FBI agent.

Around 3:56pm, I saw her pull up in her Mercedes Maybach. For some reason, even though I was sure Peel bought that for her, I felt like TQ bought it. I know I'm crazy, but when you get a nigga like mine you become that way.

I gripped the lever of my door, waiting until she got out of her car. She was taking forever, looking into her visor mirror and touching up her makeup. Hayden was a pretty girl, but her dismissal of the fact that I was TQ's girlfriend and soon to be child's mother, took away from her beauty. I didn't understand why the prettiest girls would settle for being a man's backup or second choice. It seemed like the ugly rat looking bitches had more pride in themselves.

After sliding some shades on, she got out of her car and so did I. Jogging across the street, I was right on her heels as she stepped onto the sidewalk of her apartment building. She finally stopped, and then spun around on her heels, adjusting the chain link strap on her pretty white Chanel purse. She was dressed nicely in a two-piece gray suit since she'd just come from work, and she also had on gray Christian Louboutins.

"Kimberlyn, can I help you?" she removed her expensive shades from her face.

"Listen, Hayden, I understand that you and Tarenz were friends and shit before I came along, but I'm letting you know now that the friendship is over. I applaud the fact that he decided to come to your defense regarding your domestic issues, but you need to find a new shoulder to cry on and a new dick to try to ride on. TQ should not be handling your problems, and he will not be helping you out every time you run into one. He has other things going on that he needs to handle, and you will not be throwing your shit into the mix. I am his girlfriend, not you. He is not responsible for you and the mistakes that your lovers make. If I find out that you're attempting to get him to come over here, or asking him to rescue you, I will make your life a living hell."

"He hits me up too, Kimberlyn."

"No, he doesn't. I read the text threads going all the way back to a month before I met his ass, just to be sure. Even when we broke up he didn't text you, you texted him, begging him to come over so you could give him some head."

"You don't know—"

"What is it that you said? 'TQ, I miss you, I'm craving that dick,'" I recited her text verbatim. I'd taken screenshots of all the ones I wanted, and airdropped them to myself. I knew if I texted or emailed them, he would find out.

She stared at me as her big bottom lip trembled like a baby. One tear came out of her eye, but she wiped it quickly as she stared past me into the street.

"You're right," she shook her head as she looked down.

"About what?" I frowned, a bit surprised. I was expecting a rougher rebuttal.

"About me chasing TQ. I've been wanting him for years and nothing has changed, nothing. And now me being so obsessed with him has caused me to lose my best friend."

"Don't blame that on him, blame that on your nigga."

"I don't blame him directly. I'm saying had I not been so hell bent on being with him, Peel would have never gotten violent with me, and Ingrid wouldn't have had to come over and get killed."

"You need to take responsibility, Hayden. Had you been a woman about yours and told Peel the truth, instead of leading him on, maybe you would have your best friend. But I don't care about any of that. All I care about is that you leave TQ alone. Erase him from your memories, and from your mind completely. He is gonna have his own family now. This is verbal but the next may be physical." I rubbed my small bulge because I had a little pain. I needed to calm down.

"What, what is that?" she stared down at my hand rubbing my belly.

"A baby, dummy!"

"With—" She stopped herself and looked into my eyes before turning her back to me. "I have to go, umm, I have to go." She ran inside her building.

Well at least it seems that today was beneficial for me. Slut.

Hayden Franklin

The next morning…

I threw my purse into my car, and then got in on the driver's side. Today would be the start of something new for me, and it had been a long time coming. I waved to the old lady who lived in my building, checked my side mirror, and then pulled off from the curb. Sliding my shades onto my face, I turned up the Miguel album that was currently playing in my car.

As of late, life had become too much for me. My best friend was dead, my man was too, and now the love of my life was having a baby. I chuckled angrily as I made a left turn, because I knew this would happen. I knew TQ was doing a little too much with Kimberlyn, and it would be just a matter of time before he got her pregnant or something like that. And now that she was having his baby, there was nothing I could say or do to make him leave. Even if I could though, she has his baby, which means he will always have a relationship with her.

Was I angry? Oh, I was furious, sad, and even a little bit depressed over the situation. There is truly nothing worse than watching someone you love, love someone else. He literally stepped over me to get to her, and that was a hard ass pill to swallow. It made me hate him a little at times.

But like I said, I wasn't the type of girl who drummed up plans to get a man to love me. I wasn't gonna push Kimberlyn down some stairs, or start stalking TQ in hopes that I got my way because that wouldn't work, it never did. I didn't understand those types of females because all it did was push the man further away. Not only was I not that type, I knew TQ wasn't that nigga to fuck with. He would murder my ass and no one would ever know anything. Yes, I loved him with everything in me, but I refused to risk my life for a man who would kill me and have no remorse down the line.

I continued driving and bobbing my head to Miguel's beautiful voice, as tears slipped out of my eyes. "Adorn" was playing loudly as I cried while driving. TQ and I loved this song, and every time it came on I couldn't help but to think about him. If we were in the car together we would always play it. It explained exactly how I felt about him, and I thought that was why he liked it too, but I guess I was wrong. Maybe that's why when it was over all he would say was, *that nigga can sing.* Me on the other hand, I would always comment on the fact that the lyrics spoke exactly what I was feeling. He would never respond. That nigga really had me thinking that he and I were in some secretly deep love.

It had gotten so bad for me these days that I had to sign out and delete my Instagram app because I didn't want to see Kimberlyn's posts about him or with him. Two weeks ago, she put up a picture of her sitting his lap, and it made me cry so hard that I knew something was wrong with me. It wasn't enough for me to unfollow her, because

I would still find myself typing in her name to check and see what new pictures she'd uploaded. It was to the point where I would be checking her page every morning in bed, then on my lunch break, and then right before I went to bed that night. It was as if I enjoyed being miserable, because every time I looked I would feel depressed. And to make matters worse, the only person who could make me feel better was dead. Fuck I missed Ingrid, and she died being wrapped up in my bullshit.

I made it my destination, and for old times' sake, I pulled my iPhone out and re-downloaded the Instagram app. I took deep breaths as I signed in, and then immediately went to her page like always. It took me no time because she was a suggested person already when I hit the search box. I inhaled and exhaled sharply before tapping her page, and I saw the latest picture was of her ankle. All I could see was what looked like a tattoo and an anklet. Clicking the photo to enlarge it, my heart sank when I realized she had TQ tatted on her ankle, and the picture was captioned Daddy. *Dumb ass*, I said to myself even though I didn't believe it. I would've gotten that shit too, had he been treating me the way he treated her. I almost got his name on me like a year ago, but my mother and Ingrid convinced me to wait until he and I made things official. Thank God for them.

After praying to God so that I wouldn't burst into tears, I signed back out and deleted the app. I then exited my car, hit the alarm, and went inside. The receptionist Christine smiled at me as I walked to the back, but I could tell she was wondering why I had on such casual attire. Reaching the door I was looking for, I twisted the knob and just sauntered inside.

"Ms. Franklin, is there a problem?" my boss asked.

"Not really. I just came to tell you that I quit."

Britain

I stared up at Goldie as she moved her body up and down on my dick. Gripping her small hips, I bit down on my lip to enjoy the warm, tight, feeling of her insides. She had her pretty golden hair straightened and hanging down, and she looked sexy as fuck despite her pretty light complexion being covered in sweat.

"Mmm, uuuh," she tossed her head back as she began to bounce a little faster.

"Shit, ma," I groaned, grasping her hips tighter than before.

I pressed my bottom half up into her as if I wasn't inside of her enough. When I did, the sexiest whimper burst through her full lips. A few moments later, we both exploded together. We stayed still, in the same position we'd released in as we panted heavily. I felt like I'd just ran a marathon because of all that I'd let go into her.

"Let's go shower," I said once she climbed off of me, slowly.

"Are we going somewhere?"

"Yes, but don't you shower every day anyway?" I chuckled.

"I do, but I didn't think we needed to shower together unless we were in some sort of a hurry," she exhaled, still out of breath.

"Oh, you're scared I'm gonna get back in there again, huh?" I grinned and so did she. Her face told me everything. "Come on." I pulled her towards me by the ankle, and then helped her off the bed and to the bathroom.

We entered the shower, and a good five minutes didn't even pass before I was fucking her again. Once I'd gotten my second fix, we cleaned ourselves for real, and then got out to brush our teeth at the double sinks. I made sure she kept a toothbrush and stuff here, because that was always her reason why she couldn't stay the night on school or work nights.

"May I ask where we're going?" she stared at me as she slipped her panties on.

"I will tell you once we get there."

"What if I don't want to go though? You should tell me before and let me decide if I'd like to come."

"That would be nice of me, but I don't care if you wanna go or not, you're going."

She just chuckled and pulled her short dress over her head. Her body was phenomenal, and I knew if she stood there half naked any longer, I would be ready to fuck again. Once I was dressed, I walked over to her as she tousled her hair, and bent down to kiss her soft lips a couple times. She placed her small hand into mine as she slid her feet into her sandals, and we were out the door.

About fifteen minutes later, we were pulling up to the house I'd purchased for Tekeya and I. Like I'd asked, Tekeya moved out a little less than a week after she tried to drug me. It was still crazy to me that she would do such a thing, and it almost felt unreal. Tekeya just wasn't that type of girl, so to see her take things that far was mind boggling.

"Where are we? This place is beautiful."

"This is the house I got for Tekeya."

"You mean the house you got for the both of you. The house you never moved into. Why am I here?"

"I told you she moved out and I wanted to show it to you."

"Show it to me for what?"

"See if you like it or not. If you do, then I will hold onto it until we get married or something. If you don't, I'm gonna sell it."

"Britain, whether I like it or not, I would not move in here with you if we got married. I want something another woman has never been in."

"I guess I didn't think about that. Still, come look at it." I climbed out of the car, and as I was passing the hood, I saw she was still sitting inside with her arms folded. "Get the fuck out the car!" I barked.

She sucked her teeth before exiting the vehicle like I'd asked. Entering the house, I smiled when I saw it was spotless. I'd bought furniture, well Tekeya did with my money, but I had all that removed. I gave it to some of the less fortunate Russian immigrants I knew, who needed certain things in their home.

"This is so pretty, Britain," Goldie rubbed the wall as we walked more into the home.

"I know."

We continued looking around the bottom half, before going up the stairs to see the bedrooms. I showed her all of the rooms along the way, before we reached the big ass master. Opening the door, I stepped inside and a foul smell hit me in the face like a bag of rocks.

"The fuck," I frowned as I walked further inside. I heard Goldie groan, so I knew she smelled the same thing. The sound of light sniffling caught my attention, and I looked to see it was coming from the closet. "What the hell, man!" I stormed towards it with Goldie on my heels. "Stay back!" I told her.

I was annoyed and confused because nobody knew about this house but Tekeya and a couple of her home girls. I hoped this wasn't the start of a gang or turf war because of my dad, but in case it was, I pulled my gun from my waist, before slowly pulling the doors open. When I did, Tekeya was sitting on the floor in jeans and a white top. Her jeans had a big red spot coming from the crotch, staining all the areas near it. It was a big circle on the carpet too. The smell was much stronger than before, so I knew this was where it was stemming from.

"Key, what the fuck?!" I yanked her out, and the smell got even louder making me wish I hadn't.

"What is wrong with her?" Goldie quizzed as she stared down at her in horror. In all my years of knowing Tekeya, she never looked this damn bad.

"Britain," she sang like a ghost. "Britain, I love you. Everything is all good now," she smiled up at me.

"What are you talking about? You think you can come up in my house and start your period on my floor to get me back? Key, I'm about ready to pop you!"

"Wait! Britain, I don't think that is period blood." Goldie squatted down and asked, "Were you pregnant, Tekeya?"

"Yes, but," she began shaking her head 'no' repeatedly. "Yes, but it's gone now and everything is okay. I've been sick ever since that lasagna I made, and two days ago this happened!"

"We have to get her to the hospital, Britain." Goldie stood to her feet and began dialing 911 on her iPhone.

My head was spinning at the sound of Tekeya being pregnant. I wasn't sure if I was surprised that she was pregnant, or surprised that she'd gotten pregnant by another nigga. I wasn't necessarily mad; I was just… surprised. This bitch had been full of shockers lately. I wondered what else she was hiding from me during and after the relationship. I suddenly didn't feel so bad about entertaining other women while with her.

We made it to Massachusetts General Hospital, and Tekeya was checked in and taken to the back immediately. Once they rolled her away, Goldie and I took a seat in the waiting room. I didn't really want to wait for the bitch, but Goldie did. I guess it was a woman thing because if it were just me, I might have put a bullet in her head back at the crib.

We sat there for twenty minutes before I noticed she hadn't looked my way or said a word to me since she let me know we were staying to make sure Tekeya was good.

"You okay?" I questioned, not really knowing what to say. Well I did, but I was sure if I said let's go, she'd decline.

"Shouldn't you be worrying about your baby mama."

"Baby mama? Who the fuck is my baby mama?"

"Hello!" she threw her hands up, reminding me we were in a hospital waiting on Tekeya's snake ass.

"Wait, you don't think—" I chuckled before I could even finish. "You think that's my kid she lost?" I smiled and palmed my chest.

"Well, who else's?"

"Fuck if I know! I wasn't sticking my dick in her ass! I ain't been with her for a while now, even before I started fucking with you, G."

"Yeah right. Then why is she pregnant right now? Well, why was she I mean? And she wasn't even showing so it's pretty recent."

"Well, I already told you that it wasn't my child. I don't know who she's pregnant by. Maybe since y'all are best friends you should ask her."

"Just take me home please." She stood to her feet, snatched her purse up and switched her cute ass out. I couldn't help but laugh, and I was pissed because it wasn't the time for me to be laughing.

"Shorty," I hugged her from behind and kissed her neck as we exited the hospital. "I swear I don't know who that child's father was," I chuckled some more.

"Yeah, that's why your stupid ass is laughing."

"I'm laughing because this shit is funny! You're storming out and snatching your purse like you're in some Tyler Perry film and shit, over a bitch I ain't touched in almost eight months! I'm sorry, it's comical!" I hit the alarm on my car before opening the door for her.

I got in on my side, and just stared at the side of her face for a little bit. Unfortunately, I began snickering again because her face was so knotted up it was ridiculous. I kissed her cheek and then the corner of her mouth, before making it to her lips. She didn't reciprocate at all.

"Give me a kiss."

"Take me home," she spat.

"I ain't taking yo' ass nowhere until I get a kiss. Embarrassing me in front of all of them people in the waiting room. Snatching ya purse up and shit," I chortled.

"Fine." She reached for the door to open it.

"Okay, alright! Damn!" I stopped her and cranked the car. I was really trying to be an adult and not laugh, but she was for real doing the most. I didn't feel bad because I was being honest. She didn't trust me and I didn't know what to say to make her.

I drove her home, and she hopped her ass out so quickly I could barely say bye.

Rolling down the window I yelled out "See you tomorrow, baby!" then sped off. I guess I would see what my brothers were getting into for the evening.

Fucking Tekeya, always ruining some shit. Now how the fuck am I supposed to get that stain out of my carpet?

Matikah

Ever since I found out that Dania was Isabetta's sister, work had been awkward for me. It was awkward because I didn't feel comfortable working for her knowing that my man had her sister murdered, and because Isyss was always giving me these smug looks. I felt like she was plotting on me, and I wanted to tell Lendsey, but I didn't in fear that something would happen to her. I didn't want him offing her and she wasn't even planning to do anything. That would make me feel even more awful and on edge than I already did.

I walked into my job and went behind the counter to see who I had for today. I'd been doing much better than I'd expected to be so new, and was now building a client book. Isabetta advised me that it was best to get close with the people who enjoyed my work because they would follow me if I left, and they would support me if I decided to open my own spa. I loved how helpful she was, and I appreciated that she supported me opening my own place. I feel like most bosses want you to work under them until they die.

Once I'd gotten down who I was to work on today, a smile spread across my face. Isabetta's was very popular amongst the elite people, per se. All the people that came here wore expensive clothes, drove luxury cars, and left me big tips. My favorite customers were the young girls with rich daddies, the dope boy's girlfriends, and the women who owned their own businesses. They left the best tips and always held the best conversation. I hated the housewives of rich husbands, because they were so entitled and always complaining about something. Not necessarily complaining about the service, but about their lives. One lady was upset because her husband bought her a candy apple red Mercedes, but he forgot to get glitter in the paint. Really?

As I was setting up my room for the Brazilian wax I was about to do, Isabetta walked in. We gave each other a smile, as I continued to set up.

"Matikah, I just wanted to let you know that I'm very proud of you. You've been doing a great job here, and I can't tell you how many emails I get from customers complimenting you. You have really been a great addition here, and the girls tell me all the time how much fun you are to hang out with on lunch," she chuckled and so did I.

"Thank you, and I just want to say thanks for the opportunity," I nodded.

I then began removing my bracelet so that I could put it in my purse, but she stopped me and reached for it.

"This is beautiful, Matikah."

"Thank you."

"The charms look pretty expensive. Are these real diamonds?" she inspected it.

"I believe so."

She looked up from it and smiled at me.

"Okay, who's the lucky guy? Well, I guess you're lucky too, if you get gifts like this."

"He's just my boyfriend."

"He must really love you."

"Yes, he does," I nodded, wanting to snatch the bracelet out of her hands. I knew if I did though she would look at me like I was crazy.

"LQ? What's that stand for?" she questioned and I thought I would faint.

"The-That's my grandmother's initials, umm, Luna Quintet," I lied so quickly I surprised my damn self.

"Oh yes, you did tell me you were close with her. So sweet." She handed it back to me, just as Isyss appeared in the doorway.

"Isabetta, I need some more wax, please," Isyss said while staring right into my eyes.

"Okay, I'm gonna go to the stock room. Do you need anything while I'm back there, Matikah?"

I shook my head no.

Once she left, Isyss slipped into my workroom. I stood there, not knowing what the fuck she wanted, and waiting for her weird ass to speak. Today she had strawberry orange hair, and it went well with her light skin. It was ghetto but still cute.

"I'm thinking I should tell Isabetta what I saw at the club that night," she smirked. "She's been sad still, thinking about her sister, and when I asked her what day her sister had fallen off the face of the Earth, it was ironically the day after she was at that club. I think that bit of information about the nightclub would help her look in the right direction to bring justice for her sister."

"Isyss, you don't want to do that. If I tell Lendsey—"

"Tell him what? That I'm sure he had something to do with killing Dania? What is he gonna do? You see, unlike every Tom, Dick, and Harry in Boston, I don't believe that QCF shit. Them niggas ain't a part of no damn crime family. If they were, why don't we hear about or witness the crimes?"

"So how can you say you don't believe it, but then in the same sentence accuse him of bodying Dania? It can't be both, boo."

She stared at me angrily, flaring her stupid nostrils. She was clearly dumber than she looked, and after the description I gave y'all, I'm sure you can guess that she must've looked mighty damn dumb.

"Look, regardless of what I believe, when I tell Isabetta what I saw, she's gonna be furious. Not to mention the fact that she has no idea that you're Lendsey's girlfriend."

"What do you want, Isyss?"

Well," she moved closer to me. "Why don't you come to my house tonight and I will show you what I want," she bit her lip. After glancing over her shoulder, she grabbed a wax strip and began writing on it. "Here is my address. Come over this Thursday by 9:30pm, or else. And don't be afraid to show up, Matikah. I think you may have a good time."

I took a couple deep breaths and then prepared myself for the shift. I was beyond stressed out, and I needed to calm down before I fucked a bitch's vagina up with this hot ass wax.

About four hours and some change later, it was my lunchtime. I rushed out to my car, and immediately dialed Lendsey's ass.

"What's good, ma?" he answered.

"I need to talk to you, Len, but it has to be in person."

"Okay? I will see you when you get to my home."

"No, now."

"Shorty, I'm busy right now. You can't just call me and expect me to drop what the fuck I got going, aight? What the fuck is so important?"

"Fuck you, Lendsey."

"Aight."

I hung up.

I hated how nonchalant he was whenever I got mad. It took so much to get him riled up, and I wasn't sure if it was all the weed he smoked, or if that's just how he was.

"Fuck!" I shouted.

***

I was finally off work, and speeding through Boston like a bat out of hell. I'd texted Lendsey's ass prior, and he told me he would stop through so that we could talk. Once I got inside his condo, I paced back and forth until finally his annoying ass walked through the door.

"What the hell!" I shoved him backwards. I was about to do it again but he gripped my wrists tightly in his big hands.

"We're not about to go there, Matikah. Sit yo' ass down and act like you got some fuckin' sense, shorty. My time is valuable, so talk!" he barked, scaring me a little.

"This girl at work, she's threatening to tell Isabetta what she saw!"

"First, let's stop yelling, and secondly, what did she see?" he plopped down on the couch, pulling a blunt from behind his ear. I snatched it from his lips before he could light it, but when he gave me that death stare, I gave it back.

"She was at the club the night Dania was acting crazy. She's gonna tell my boss, you know, Dania's fuckin' sister, about what happened! She's gonna tell her that it was the night before Dania went missing."

"What's her name?"

"Isyss. Isyss Pearson."

"Okay," he nodded as he stood up, still smoking the blunt.

"Wait, so what are you gonna do?"

"Take care of everything. You wanna hit this?" he reached the blunt out to me.

"Lendsey! Stop being that way!"

"Fuck do you want? For me to get upset? Yell? Throw shit? For what? What will that solve? And you think some little bitch who waxes hoes' pussies is about to have me up in arms? You must've forgotten who the fuck I am, Matikah!"

"I just—"

"I got it shorty, relax."

"I'm gonna go shower." I got up off the couch and headed to the bathroom, but I noticed he was going towards the door. "Where are you going?"

"Back to work. I have to process some shit and make some calls."

"For Isyss?"

"Who?"

"Lendsey!"

"Oh, that little bitch. Nah, I'm going to handle actual business. I will holler at her though, I promise. Go shower, I will bring food when I come. I want some head too," he flashed his gorgeous smile, while holding his blunt between his fingers. He was so rugged and sexy.

"I guess my head game has gotten better," I smirked.

"Shorty, you could suck a banana through a stir straw," he took a pull, while wearing a serious expression.

"You're disgusting," I chuckled.

"Pussy, too. I need that, I don't know which is better with you."

"Boy, leave!" I slipped into the bathroom.

I prayed to God my annoying ass sexy boyfriend would come through. He'd already slipped up and forgot to tell me Dania and Isabetta were sisters. He'd better be on his toes from here on out though.

CHAPTER TEN

Rhys

I'd just come from handling some nigga for my father, so I was at my parents' house to collect the other half of my payment. Even though I was his son, he still treated me like some random nigga he hired. He only paid me half before the job, and half after it was done. I mean I understood that business was business, but I just didn't like that he saw my brothers and I as just some other niggas. We were only his sons when he wanted to boast to his friends about his lineage.

For some reason, having four sons was commendable. My mom said he'd always been that way, because he'd tell her all the time how he needed sons to continue his legacy. She said when their first child turned out to be a girl, he was furious and spent three months with other women because he thought something was wrong with my mother. He told me something was wrong with Summer when she had Bryleigh, so I knew it was true. My mom only told me this information, and made sure to make me swear I would never tell my siblings, especially Saya. Funny enough, although disappointed upon her arrival, my dad treated Saya like gold. My mother said she thanked God every night that he blessed her with four boys after Saya, but a part of me wishes she had divorced my father's ungrateful ass and given me a different dad.

"I'm here for the other half," I walked into his office.

He gestured for me to sit down as he continued his phone conversation. It sounded as if he was setting up a card game or a party. Whichever it was, I knew he was gonna make some money from it; he and his friend Danil Smirnov, a known illegal gambler. That nigga made 100,000 in one night from gambling, but that was some years back. These days he stayed losing and asking my dad for a loan.

"Okay, I'm sorry, son, what are you here for again?"

"My payment, Pop. Jahlil Sanders is a dead man, like you asked." I slid the yellow envelope to him, which contained the boy's ear.

"Great."

He pulled out his big notebook of checks and began writing one out, catching me off guard. I wasn't taking any damn checks. It's not like he wasn't good for it, I just didn't fuck with that shit.

"Nah, I need cash."

"I only have $30,000 in cash right now, Rhys. What, you don't trust me?" He stood up and walked over to his bar.

"I didn't say that, I just prefer cash. I want cash."

"I have $30,000 for you right now, but that's it." He poured some liquor into his glass.

"I need the full amount due in cash right now, or I'm not doing anymore jobs for you."

"Oh really? And how do you expect to make a living if you don't work within the family?"

"Other niggas know who I am. I will work for another family."

"Oh really? Who? The Italians? You think they're gonna trust you? Some blue-eyed Russian and black kid who won't even work for his own father?" he laughed as he swished his drink and ice around. "Even if they did take you, Boston is mine so you'd have to leave the state to find them."

"Dad, I'm exhausted and I have other shit going on. I just want to get my money and go home to get some sleep."

"Go home to that whore you're fucking?" he grinned. I hopped up fast as fuck and placed my gun to his chin. He continued smiling and laughing, but my angry facial expression didn't budge. "You're gonna kill me, Rhys? Really?" he chuckled. I stared into his matching blue eyes, wanting to blow his brains through the top of his skull.

"Just get me my money." I put my gun away.

He shook his head while chuckling, as he walked over to his safe. He typed in the code, and tossed me a bag of money. I looked through it right then and saw it was only $30,000.

"I will get you the other twenty by tomorrow afternoon. A courier will bring it so it won't be an inconvenience."

I just turned on my heels and left the room. As I passed my mother's office, I glanced inside to see Indiya sitting there. Watching her type on the computer made me smile. I convinced my mom to allow Indiya to assist her and Saya with their business. Right now she was in charge of booking the hotel suites for the girls. It wasn't much, but it paid her nicely so she was satisfied.

"I'm almost ready," she smiled.

"Who said you were coming home with me?" I asked as I entered the office fully.

"I did." I watched her finish up, and then she stood to her feet to grab her stuff. "Thank you for this fancy briefcase. I don't have much to put in it, but I will figure out some ways to make it useful," she giggled. Shorty was sexy as hell from the top of her head to the tip of her toes. But aside from her beauty, I was falling for her personality. She wasn't on that victim shit that Summer stayed on.

"You're welcome."

We walked out hand in hand, but then I heard a familiar voice coming down the hallway. My brows furrowed upon seeing my baby girl walking in between my mother and Summer.

"Daddy!" she shouted and ran when she saw me.

"Hey, Bry!" I scooped her up and she hugged my neck tightly like always. Closing my eyes, I hugged her small frame. I loved my daughter more than anything, which is why I couldn't understand how my dad could act the way he did towards us.

"I missed you, Daddy! Can I come home with you?"

"I thought you were here to see me, Bry?" my mom chimed in, laughing.

"Yes, but my Daddy is here so he can take me home. I will see you next week, Granny."

"No Bry, you'll hurt your grandmother's feelings. I will have you this weekend, remember?" I kissed her face. The whole time my mother, Bryleigh, and I interacted, Summer just glared at Indiya.

"Okay." She dropped her head. Quickly picking it back up, she looked down at Indiya. "Hi, I'm Bryleigh Quinton."

"Hi Bryleigh, I've heard so much about you. I'm Indiya."

"Indiya! My mommy told her friend on the phone that you and my daddy fuck."

Everyone dropped their jaws, including me when those words left her lips. I'd told Summer on countless occasions to make sure Bryleigh wasn't listening to her conversations, and she never would take that extra step.

"Bryleigh, don't say that word, baby," I rubbed her back. She looked at me sadly, and I could tell she didn't know what she said was wrong. My daughter was very well behaved and she never said things that she thought were bad. "It's cool, just don't say it again, alright?" She nodded.

I kissed her cheek and placed her to her feet. She walked up to Indiya and stuck her hand out to shake it, but Summer snatched her away with the quickness. I swear these days I couldn't stand Summer. It's crazy because some months back I was dumb for her psycho ass.

"Well, Ma, we're about to leave," I said.

"Okay sweetie, bye Indiya," she responded before she led Bryleigh away to go have a snack.

Indiya and I walked hand in hand down the hall, and I could feel Summer watching me as she slowly followed behind my mother and daughter. I had no interest in speaking to her in this moment, or any other moment for that matter. I still loved her, but I would be lying if I said my love wasn't dwindling. I would also be lying if I said I didn't have strong feelings for Indiya.

"That was weird," Indiya sighed when we got into my car.

"I know, but don't trip off that shit, shorty."

She leaned over, turned me to face her, then pressed her soft lips against mine. We sat there tonguing it up for a little while, and then I finally sped out, ready to fuck. I got to my home fast as hell, and wasted no time getting up into my condo.

As we were kissing hungrily and undressing each other, the anticipation of being inside of her continued to build. It was almost like I was addicted to her, and honestly I'd never felt this way about any woman. Indiya was just different, and I didn't know if it was a good thing or a bad thing. Summer was perfect despite her insecurities, but so was Indiya.

"Rhys," she called my name lightly once we fell onto the bed. I was tugging her lace panties down her smooth thighs.

"What's up?"

"Your mother asked me if I was your girlfriend today, and I didn't know what to say. The other day when I went to the grocery store, a guy asked me if I had a boyfriend and again I didn't know what to say."

We stared at each other for a couple of seconds, before she began smiling. I had no idea what the fuck we were talking about, so I was hoping she was going to continue and elaborate.

"I forgot men don't read between the lines," she sighed. "What are we? I know I said I would never ask, but I need to know what to say when I'm asked these questions."

I planted kisses up her flat stomach until I reached her collarbone. I then trailed my lips from her neck, to her cheek, and then her lips.

"You tell my mother yes, and any niggas that ask you, yes as well." I pinned her hands behind her head. I couldn't help but smile upon seeing that huge grin on her face when she heard my answer.

"Okay, boyfriend," she giggled.

"Silly."

I slid my tongue into her mouth, before going back down and handling business.

Goldie

A couple days later…

"What do you think about this one?" I held up a tube top for Kimberlyn to see. We were at Copley Place, shopping.

"Yes, that's very cute. I want one, it will give me motivation to get fit after the baby."

Her stomach was still small even though she was six months along. I thought it would be far out, but it wasn't much really. She said her grandmother told her carrying small ran in the family, so I guess this was normal for them. If she wore a shirt that was big enough, you wouldn't know she was pregnant at all.

After getting what we wanted, we went to the front to ring up, and then headed to Louis Vuitton, Jimmy Choo, and Neiman Marcus.

"I can't believe I bought shoes from Jimmy's, I feel like I should return them," I chuckled as we walked through the mall to get to the car.

"No, don't. They're cute and every girl deserves at least one pair of expensive shoes. Plus, it's not like Britain can manage your money, it's in *your* account."

"True. Speaking of Britain, I haven't talked to him in a couple days."

"Why?" she frowned as we exited the huge mall finally.

"Because he got his ex pregnant. He claims he hasn't slept with her in months, but we all know that ain't true."

"We do?"

"Yes, we do," I nodded, not wanting to hear her take his side. A part of me felt like I jumped the gun before I actually had a chance to think about it. However, I was the type of person who hated to be wrong, so I didn't want to think about it now that I had cut him off.

"Has he texted or called you?" She hit the alarm on her car as we neared it inside of the fairly empty parking structure. It was a Wednesday evening so there wasn't a crowd here.

"Yes he has, but I don't answer."

We placed our bags into the trunk of the car, and then got inside. She cut the air on, but since it was still hot, I rolled my window down to let some of the heat out. It was super cold outside, but I guess all of that walking had me burning up.

POP! POP!

A body dropped to the floor right next to Kimberlyn's car, and when I peeked out, I saw a guy groaning on the floor with a knife in his hand. As soon as I looked the other way to see who had shot him, some men in a black truck hopped out, scooped him up, and carried him back to the truck before peeling off. Blood was all over the parking space next to us, and I was scared out of my mind.

Suddenly, Kimberlyn's phone rang, and she was talking for a little bit with the person on the other line. I was making sure no one else was gonna run up by us, and I was hoping that truck of killers was gone as well.

"Who was that?" I asked once she hung up and began pulling out.

"TQ. He said Gang hired someone to stab me in the stomach. You know the brothers have people watching us, so that's who shot him before he could attack I'm assuming."

"What the fuck is wrong with Gang?"

"No idea," she shook her head as she continued out. Stuff was getting a little bit too real for me right now. Was I really about that life?

Kimberlyn dropped me off at my new condo, and as soon as I got in, I made me some food. Before I could even finish it, I was throwing it all up in the trashcan. This had been happening for the past few days. The first time was when I made Britain take me home after the hospital, and it'd been happening ever since.

After brushing my teeth and downing some water, I pulled out the pregnancy test that I'd purchased this morning when Kimberlyn and I were in CVS. After peeing on it, I set it on a paper towel, washed my hands, and then turned on a timer so I would know when to look. While I waited, I decided to text Britain since I kind of missed him.

Me: *Hi*

Baby: *Oh now you know me?*

Me: *Yes... lol. You should come over. I will cook for you.*

Baby: *If I have the time.*

***Me:** Fine.*

***Baby:** What time?*

I smiled before responding.

***Me:** It's 6pm now, so 8pm.*

***Baby:** Okay.*

My timer went off, so I stopped it before rising to my feet. I walked slowly as if there was an electric chair waiting for me. Entering the bathroom with my eyes closed, I took a good deep breath before opening them. I picked the test up, and just stared at the word pregnant for decades it seemed. I took another one to be sure, and when it came back the same, I just laid it next to the other.

After cleaning my hands again, I went to the kitchen and began preparing some food for Britain. I told him my specialty was hot wings, and he claimed that he loved spicy food so I wanted to make them. I warned his ass that they were extremely hot, but he acted as if I was the funniest person in the world.

About an hour later, I heard some keys in the door, so I knew it was him coming in. When I saw his face, I gave him a light smile, and then told him to sit down at the bar in my kitchen. I loved my new condo because it was spacious, beautiful, and in a quiet ass neighborhood. It was definitely a huge ass upgrade from my beat up ass apartment.

"What are you making?" he wiggled his nose, and I knew it was because of all the spices. His ass was about to pass out.

"My wings that I promised you."

"Oh, the ones that you claim are so damn hot," he scoffed and texted something on his phone.

"How many?" I questioned, ignoring the fact that he was underestimating my food.

"I will start with ten."

"Britain, I'm telling you they're really hot baby. Why don't you start with four?"

"Nah, five." He just had to make his own choices.

I rolled my eyes and placed the five wings onto the plate. I slid the plate in front of him, and then poured him a glass of milk because I was sure he would need it. He laughed when I did that. Placing my elbows on the island, I leaned in to watch him eat the food. I tried to hold in my laughter as he started sniffling and licking his full lips. I knew they were burning him up, but he wasn't gonna say anything. Once he reached for the milk, I slid it towards me, and away from him.

"Shorty, give me the milk."

"You need it?" I grinned.

"Yes I need it, what the fuck did you put on these damn wings?"

"Barbecue sauce, Sriracha, ground habanero, jalapeño relish, capsaicin, and a secret sauce that includes ghost peppers," I smiled as he stared at me panting like a dog.

"The milk!"

"Say the magic wooorrddd," I chuckled as he rose to his feet to come around the corner of the island.

"Shorty, give me the fucking milk."

"That's not the right word, Britain. You have more manners than that, don't you?"

"Goldie, shorty, please," he stared down at me. His deep blue eyes were watery, and he looked so adorable, causing me to give in. "Thank you." He gulped it down. Once he was finished, I turned the water on so he could wash his hands, and then led him to the bathroom.

"Come in," I waved him since he was stuck at the doorway.

"What?"

"I took these today," I said in a low tone, not knowing how he would react.

"You're pregnant?" I just nodded. "Come here." He pulled me in and kissed my lips gently. His were red and they burned mine a little, but I didn't care. We continued to kiss for a little while, but then we pulled away.

"This is good, right?" I smiled.

"Yeah, this is good."

"I'm sorry for not believing that Tekeya wasn't pregnant by you." I hugged his torso and stared up into his face.

"It's cool, but you have to trust me from now on, ma."

"I do, baby daddy," I grinned and so did he before he kissed me.

"Now come on, I have to finish those wings or I'm gonna feel like bitch." He took my hand into his as we laughed our way back to the itchen.

I guess I was stuck with his sexy ass now.

At the moment, Kimberlyn and I were at my home in Bridgeport, on Old Battery Road. I needed to get away so that I could think without people being in my face and ear. I damn sure wasn't about to leave my girl at home, so I packed her up to come with me. It was the weekend anyway, so it wasn't like she had class or anything. All she needed to bring was that damn laptop that she worked on and she'd be good.

When I got back to Boston, and even while I was out here in Bridgeport, I would have to make arrangements to kill Gang. It was nothing for me to pop the nigga; shit, I would have done it some time back to be perfectly honest. The problem was my father. Gang was my dad's pride and joy because he made him so much money. See, usually there was no way my dad would allow a distributor to ask him of so many favors. When he told my dad that he would find someone else to get product from, my father would have put a bullet in him. But money was my father's second love, crime being his first, so until he found another nigga in Boston who could push as much weight as Gang, he wasn't touching him. Gang knew that too, because Stony Quinton was not the nigga to threaten like Gang had done in a sense.

There lied the problem. Stony wasn't your typical father, so the fact that Gang had hired someone to stab Kimberlyn only enough to kill my child, wasn't reason enough for me to kill Gang in my dad's eyes. So by saying that, me murdering him would definitely cause some shit between he and I. Sometimes I got in my feelings and wished I had a father who cared more about his real family than the Quinton Crime Family, but then I would just suck it up. The time to cry about it had passed me up, and now that I was a grown ass man, and about to have a family, I could no longer pine for my father's love. And frankly, I didn't even think I really wanted it.

Gang had to die, and he was going to die, I just had to make sure that I did it right. Killing him was gonna be harder than killing Peel, just because of the simple fact that Peel was more in tune with where he came from. What I mean by that is, Peel didn't travel with security 24/7. Now neither did my brothers and I, because honestly, no one was dumb enough. But in settings where there would be a lot of people, we did bulk up. Gang on the other hand, had security wherever he went, and I really couldn't blame him. Many niggas in Boston were jealous of him and Peel, just like they were of my brothers and I. Gang had been shot and set up on plenty of occasions, but because of who my dad knows and has on payroll, nothing ever stuck.

That brings on the real question I had to ask myself: was I prepared to deal with my father? Would he remove me from the family? Would he declare me an enemy? And if so, would my brothers rock with me or him? My head was hurting just from thinking about all of this. It would be easy for me to let Gang live and continue to protect Kimberlyn, but I couldn't. Nothing in me would allow this man who attempted to harm my child over some pussy, to live. He had to die, and there was no way around the shit. I would die protecting mine.

As I stared out of the big window of my bedroom, looking at the huge forest like backyard of mine, Kimberlyn walked in, coming from the shower. She had on one of my plush white robes, and it was funny to see how loosely it hung off of her petite frame. She gave me a smile, a big one like always, and then removed the robe to begin putting some lotion from a jar on her body. While watching her, an idea hit me.

"Let me take some pictures of you baby," I said, getting up off the bed.

"Pictures?" she chuckled as I pulled my camera from under the bed.

Flying planes wasn't the only thing I loved, I also enjoyed taking photographs. My maternal grandfather made his living taking portraits for families, babies, pets, whoever needed a picture. Growing up, whenever my mother would either leave my dad because she caught him with another mistress, or had to be away from him for legal reasons, we would visit my grandpa in Harlem. I was so fascinated by his camera, that he would spend hours showing me and telling me how to get the perfect picture. And while my brothers and sister would be playing or stuffing their faces with my grandmother's cooking, I would be snapping photos like crazy. Now that I was so busy, I rarely found time to do it. But seeing my shorty with her stomach, looking all beautiful and shit, it seemed to be the perfect occasion. It was something I wanted to capture.

"Do you know how to use that?" she asked when she saw me pull it out.

"Hell yeah I do. My grandfather got me into photography when I was like seven years old, and I've been doing it ever since. Last time was before I met you though, so I want to end that drought. I hope it's charged."

"What should I do?"

"You have a short top to put on? Or can you just cover yourself with your arms?"

"What about this?" she held up a red lace lingerie set.

I nodded to give my approval, and then waited for her to put on the bra and panties. She grabbed the matching short silk robe as well, leaving it open, and then sat on the window seat in the bedroom. I smiled as she sat there innocently, waiting for me to direct her.

"Tilt your head back, and let your hair fall and shit," I said, looking through the camera viewer.

She did as I asked, and the sun setting on the backyard with her by the window was perfect. She continued to give me very poetic poses, some with her hand on her stomach, some with her staring out of the window, and even some standing up. I could take pictures of her all day, and seeing my initials tatted on her ankle made the view even better.

When we were done, I showed her some of the photos, and then helped her down off the window. I then led her to the bed, and assisted her in removing the lingerie while kissing her.

Once she was finally naked, I undressed myself, and since I was only in my boxers it took no time. Climbing in between her legs, I made sure not to press myself against her, before sliding inside. Holding her face in my hands, I began tonguing her down as I continued to glide in and out of her walls. As I made love to her, I thought about our relationship and how in order for it to prosper, Gang would have to die. If my father declared me a foe, then it would all be worth it.

I felt her coat my dick, which only made what I was feeling even more intense. The feeling of her small hands caressing my biceps as I sucked on her lips, had my dick getting harder by the second. This shit was like an outer body experience almost.

"Mmm, uuuh," she threw her head back, pressing it into the pillow as I invaded her body time and time again.

Placing her legs in the nooks of my arms, I slammed into her, making her cry out loudly across the huge home. A moan or two even slipped out of my mouth as I pounded between her hips. Moments later, I was filling her up and groaning like an animal. I fell down next to her, and she climbed on top of me to lay her head on my chest.

"I know you went to Hayden's," I rubbed her back. She picked her head up off of my chest and looked into my face, causing me to laugh. "It's cool, shorty, just don't converse with her."

"As long as she converses with you, I will be conversing with her."

"She won't be conversing with me anymore, so calm your little ass down."

"You killed her?"

"No, I didn't. But she won't be in our lives any longer, aight?" she nodded and laid her head back down on my chest.

Now that Hayden was gone in a sense, all I had to do was get rid of Gang. I wished that would be the end, but I knew it would only be the beginning.

Saadiq "Gang" Ronson

Two weeks later...

"I didn't like what you were saying on the phone, Jayce." I sipped my glass of whiskey. It was strong as hell right now, and every time I took a sip, it was like a punch to the chest.

Jayce called me last week crying like a little bitch, saying TQ was on to him. It annoyed me to the depths of my soul when niggas acted like the Quintons ran shit around here. Yeah they had clout, but so did I, and I was the face of Boston. When niggas came here, I was the nigga they heard about other than Stony. Shit, Stony was the only reason TQ, Rhys, Lendsey, and Britain were even able to make a name for themselves. I worked my ass off to get the respect that I have as Gang. I didn't ride my father's coattails like them bitches. I was tired of everybody downing my achievements whenever the Quintons were brought up.

To make matters worse, Kimberlyn being stolen from me was like a shot heard around the world. It made me regret the fact that I'd shown her off to everyone, just for her to be on TQ's arm now. You would think she'd be getting called a hoe everywhere she went, but no, niggas were too scared to come at her like that because of TQ. I hated that people acted as if Kimberlyn was higher than me now, like she had married a king or something. If it weren't for me she wouldn't have even met TQ. She was a regular girl from Roxbury, and although she was pretty, her and TQ would have never crossed paths had I not brought her into my upscale circle. My thoughts caused me to grind my teeth and squeeze my glass.

"Gang! Man snap out of it!" Jayce shouted as he paced my study.

"I know TQ is after me."

"Yeah, because the nigga you hired to abort Kimberlyn's baby failed! I told you it wasn't gonna be that easy to just run up on her because of what Monica did!" Jayce barked.

The mention of Monica gave me a sharp pain in my chest. I missed shorty like crazy, and it made me wish I could go back and spend more time with her.

I looked over to Jayce with a disgusted expression.

He was dumb and meant nothing to me. I was simply using him to murder TQ. Once he was dead, I would make it look like Jayce did it, and TQ's brothers would murk his ass. Jayce believed that if he helped me he would assume Peel's position, but that couldn't be further from the truth. Why the fuck would I recruit a nigga like him to run my empire? TQ was this nigga's best friend, and Stony had done a lot for this nigga, but because he couldn't get his way he was willing to betray them. He couldn't be trusted, and once TQ was in the grave, and Kimberlyn was in my bed, I would throw Jayce into the lion's den, or the Quinton's den. I laughed to myself before refilling my glass. Plus, I was already talking to another cat about taking Peel's place, unbeknownst to Jayce.

"This is the plan, Jayce. I want you to be by me at all times, and when I need you, you will come out and help me. TQ is no dummy, and I know he's plotting on me right now. What I need—"

"We need more people, Gang, especially if his brothers get involved!"

"You got one more time to yell before I put a cap in yo' ass." I was starting to think it was a bad idea to work with him because he was acting extremely fickle right now. "Get back close with him, and try to get some details on what he has planned for me. Make it seem like you want to help. When that happens, we will take over the situation and murk him."

"Gang—"

"Okay?" I stared into his eyes.

"Aight. And what about Kimberlyn? She's gonna have his kid and I don't know how easily she will warm up to you, Gang."

"Kimberlyn is disloyal, and can be easily swayed. She goes whichever way the damn wind blows, and once her child's father is in the ground, she won't even think about him anymore."

"Are you sure?"

"I know Kimberlyn better than anybody, and if she would up and leave me in one damn night for another nigga, do you honestly think she's gonna stay in the house mourning TQ?" I chuckled at the thought.

"Why do you even want the bitch then? If you know she's not loyal, that means she may betray you again."

"That won't happen because this time I'm gonna get some pussy, and also, I'm gonna have to be a little more controlling. My father always said, if you want a woman to behave you have to use your fists. And in addition to that, I'm gonna keep that ass barefoot and pregnant."

"I mean I get it, but I don't know if his brothers will allow you to mistreat her like that. They're dating her friends and her friends won't allow it for sure."

"Them niggas won't care about her once they see how quickly she hops onto another dick. And I'll be cutting her off from Matikah and Goldie."

"Gang, man, I don't—"

"Why the fuck are you so worried about how I'm gonna keep Kimberlyn? You wanna fuck her or something? Because if not, I don't see how this has anything to do with you!"

"You're right, it doesn't. I was just trying to make sure you had everything figured out. That would be fucked up if you did all this and still didn't get the girl."

"I'm doing this for her, *and* for Peel."

"I feel—"

"Excuse me, Mr. Ronson, there is a woman here to see you," my housekeeper Roberta peeked her head into the study.

"Did she give a name or do you want me to guess who the fuck it is?"

"She-she said her name was Tekeya Mitchell, sir."

I just nodded to say it was okay for her to bring Tekeya in. I could only imagine why she was here, but Peel did tell me he fucked her a couple of times. He said she liked to pretend it was only one time that she remembered, but he smashed a good three times. She finally walked into the study looking like she was scared to speak. It was hilarious because Tekeya was known to be sexy and loud all the damn time. Niggas hated on Britain for bagging her, but we were all thankful we dodged the headache she was to him. I would've been broken my foot off in her ass.

"Why are you here, ma?"

"I need your help and advice."

"With?" I gestured for her to sit on the leather sofa that Jayce was on.

"I need to get back at Britain for what he's done to me."

"Well you've come to the right place, shorty. Taking down a Quinton is my new hobby and specialty," I smiled, prompting a smirk to creep across her face.

"My brother is in law enforcement if that helps."

"Really?" I cheesed. "Continue."

Jayce just sat there looking like a deer in headlights. It was cool though, because soon enough he'd be dead too.

CHAPTER ELEVEN

Lendsey

I opened the fridge to see if there was something to drink. I saw a water bottle, but because the whole damn fridge was disgusting and smelled like old broccoli, I opted out of drinking it. I'd been in this house for a damn hour, and was getting restless. I wasn't gonna leave until I accomplished what I came to do though. Slamming the fridge closed, I went to sit down in the dark hallway to check my texts.

Ever since I'd had Dania murdered, my phone hasn't been blowing up as much, and I must say I enjoyed it. Calling and texting me nonstop was something I despised, and I never understood it. If I didn't answer the first time, why would I answer the twentieth? Dania was the queen of that shit, and wouldn't let up until I answered. Was I sad that she was dead? In a sense, only because I'd known her for such a long time, and at one point she and I were cool. I knew that if I didn't get rid of her though, I would possibly lose Matikah, and that wasn't happening again.

After responding to a few home girls and homies, I put my phone up. I kept the conversations platonic, because one, I wasn't going down that road again, and two, because Matikah demanded that she have my password. She even had her fingerprint listed as well in my phone. I didn't even know two prints could be assigned to one phone until she requested for that shit to be done. My shorty was crazy, but I wasn't tripping. That's what my ass gets for being a dummy with Dania.

I heard keys jingling in the door, so I slowly stood to my feet. She cut the lights on in the living room, sighed, and then cut them back off. As she was walking towards me in the dark hallway, I held my breath so that she wouldn't suspect anything while she was so far away from me.

"Ah!" she jumped once she got close enough to see me in the pitch-black hallway.

"Isyss," I growled as I yanked her back to me by the arm.

I turned her to face me, and then wrapped my hands around her neck. Her eyes almost bulged out of her head as I cut off her circulation like it was nothing. I mean it was a piece of cake since she was about one hundred pounds soaking wet. She squirmed and scratched at my hands, but my gloves were providing one hell of a protective barrier.

"Matikah told me your views on my brothers and I. We were just some myths you said, right? Or something like that. We actually prefer to keep it that way, Isyss. The only people who really know the truth are our victims, like you," I spoke to her calmly, as if we were having cups of tea and conversation.

Her flailing was starting to slow down tremendously as I looked around, taking in what I could see in the dark. I was getting bored, and wanted her to die already. Taking one hand off of her throat, I pulled out my switchblade and jammed it into her midsection as I squeezed harder on her neck. Her eyes got even bigger as she began to choke on her own blood. Her eyelids began to go up and down very slowly as blood spilled between her lips, just before she took her last breath… or attempted to. I dropped her ass to the floor, and stepped over her like she was nothing. I exited her apartment through the back window, and climbed down the side before darting out.

One the way home, I lit a blunt, rolled my windows all the way down, and turned up the Yo Gotti album I was listening to. I was feeling good right now, and not because I'd just strangled a bitch in her apartment either. But because, right now, everything in my life was going good. I had money, a shorty I loved, and no crazy hoes trying to break me down. I took a big pull on the blunt just to celebrate everything, as I drove up to my condo.

When I walked inside, I smelled some sort of sweet candle, which made me smile. Making my way to the bathroom, I removed my hoodie and t-shirt in one motion, before cutting on the shower. I then removed everything else, and hopped in to scrub myself down. After I got out, I wrapped a towel around my waist, and padded to the bedroom.

The door was cracked, so I pushed it all the way open to see Matikah lying in the middle of the bed, wearing a very sexy pink number. It was so damn see-through and small, that she might as well have been naked. She tousled her curly hair to the other side while licking her lips, as I removed my towel. Once it hit the floor, I began damn near ripping her negligée off.

"And you wonder why I can't stop fucking you," I said in a low tone as I eyed her perfect breasts.

I immediately took her nipple into my mouth and began sucking as if my life depended on it. She caressed my hair while moaning, as I tugged the suit past her ass and hips. We were about to make a baby tonight, I could feel that shit. I was high as a muthafucka too, which meant I was gonna be ready for that back to back.

Pushing her onto her back, I spread her legs and kissed from her ankles all the way down to her center. After inhaling her scent, I pressed her legs into her stomach, and began sucking her clit hungrily as she whimpered.

I used to think I didn't like eating pussy, but I think it was because I only fucked with hoes, and I couldn't imagine putting my mouth down there. I'd only eaten out three women and that was during my early years before TQ went in on my ass, saying I wasn't supposed to munch on every bitch I fucked. I was sixteen… give me a break. Anyway, with Matikah I enjoyed the shit as if it were my favorite pastime.

"Baby, mmm, uuuh!" she cried as she released for the third time. I'd gotten so lost that I hadn't even realized how long I'd been down there.

I gave her one more peck between the legs, before she pushed me onto my back to take me into her mouth. Matikah had the jaws of life, and the shit had me wondering if she was sucking other dicks while we were broken up. She claimed it was because she enjoyed it, and I accepted that, because thinking otherwise would drive me insane.

"Fuck," I groaned as I palmed the back of her head. She was slobbing me up like a beast, and soon enough, I was exploding. "Baby,

I love you," I panted as she stood to her feet and tried to mount me. "Nah, face down, ass up," I flipped her over, as she giggled seductively.

Gripping her hips, I slid into her from behind and went in. The weed mixed with her phenomenal pussy had me about to cry in a minute, and I had to keep slowing down so I wouldn't nut early. She had to get hers first. I wound my hips slowly as I tapped her spot, making her coo and cry. Running my hand down her sweaty back, I trailed it to her perfectly round ass to grip it. Giving it a good smack, I sped up and overestimated my stamina because I came all in her just as she released on me. I was so out of breath as I bent down to kiss her neck and back.

"Don't be gripping my dick like that, shorty," I taunted and fell to the side.

"You like it," she smiled as she snuggled up to me.

I lit another blunt that she'd pre rolled for me, and we smoked, talked, and fucked until the morning. She made us breakfast once the sun came up, and then we finally fell asleep.

See what I meant about life being good?

Summer

Some weeks later…

Hakim and I had been taking it slow, but I think now I was ready to move to that next step; especially since Rhys had a girlfriend. I asked Bryleigh some questions and she said, "they do what you and Daddy used to, Mommy". Those were her words verbatim. Hearing her say that had my blood boiling, but it gave me the motivation I needed to move on with Hakim. I wanted to be with Hakim anyway.

"Sweetie, are you okay?" Hakim asked once he watched me down my third glass of the $400 Japanese liquor we'd ordered.

"Yes, I'm great. Do I seem like I'm bothered?" I frowned.

"Yeah, I've been talking to you and you haven't said a word. I even waved my hand in front of your eyes, but you didn't respond."

"I'm sorry. I'm just- Can I be honest?"

"Of course."

"My ex has a new girlfriend, and she's a former escort. Shoot, she may still be one. I just don't like that she's around my daughter."

"Have you met her?"

"Briefly."

"Maybe you should try to meet her for real, and then see if you actually like her. She may be a nice person; her occupation really doesn't have anything to do with it."

"Is that what you think? What kind of woman sells her body? She can't be that great."

"I get that part, it's definitely not the best job. But still I think your ex has pretty good taste in women, don't you?" he flashed his sexy smile.

"I mean, I guess I am a great catch."

"You really are, ma."

I blushed just as the waitress set our sushi dishes down. After praying, we both dug in and even fed each other here and there. I always wanted to do that, but Rhys hated it. He was just too thugged out for some stuff. I used to think it was funny, but now I hated everything about him. As much as I loathed him, I couldn't get his stupid whack ass off of my mind. It was really bad tonight because Bryleigh was over there.

Hakim and I finished dinner, and afterwards, we went straight to his place in Jamaica Plain. Once inside, he opened some wine and we just sat there sipping and staring off. We hadn't had sex yet, and I wasn't used to being the initiator. Rhys always pounced on me whenever he had a chance to, so I had no idea how to make a move.

"So tonight was good, it was nice," I smiled.

"Yeah, it was."

"How do you end such a perfect night?" I half smiled at him, hoping I looked somewhat seductive.

"Nothing like a good movie," he stretched, and then burst into laughter. "I'm kidding Summer, come here." He pulled me closer to him.

We began kissing, and I just closed my eyes because I loved the feeling of his soft lips. I couldn't take it anymore, so I began unbuttoning his dress shirt, and he followed suit by unzipping my dress. I stood up to step out of it, and enjoyed seeing his eyes light up upon seeing my half naked body. Once my panties were off, he grabbed me by the waist and sat me down, before getting onto the floor to tease my center with his tongue.

"Hakim," I moaned as he began to suck my button. "Mmm, shit."

His hands rubbed up and down my thighs as he feasted, and soon enough, I was quivering from releasing. That didn't stop him, though. He kept attacking my pussy like he'd been dreaming of this day, and I was loving every minute of it. I exploded again, and finally he pulled away. Rising to his feet, he undressed himself while watching me closely. I was on pins and needles waiting to see the size of his dick because I knew it was big. I was right too. As soon as it was released, he stroked it slowly while walking towards me. I laid on my back because I wasn't sucking dick tonight, well not his anyway. I was used to giving Rhys head so it was nothing, but a new dick would take me some time. He paused for a second, but then just went with the flow, climbing on top of me on the sofa.

"You good?" he asked as he opened the condom he had and rolled it down. I just nodded because I was soaking wet, and just ready to fuck. In a minute I was gonna be texting Rhys.

"Uuuh oooh," I moaned out as he pushed himself inside of me. "Go deeper," I coached him and spread my legs wider. I'd been deprived all this time.

"Damn, Summer," he bit down on his lip as he moved in and out of me slowly.

We started kissing as groped my breasts and made love to me. I didn't want to make love, but at least I was getting sex so I wasn't going to complain. He wasn't getting deep enough, so gripped his ass and began pressing him inside of me. He moved my hands and pressed them above my head so quickly I almost got whiplash.

"You want it rough you little hoe?" he asked, catching me off guard.

"I—" Before I could finish, he flipped me onto all fours with my top half hanging over the couch's arm.

He slid into me instantaneously, and began ramming into me with power and force. He was fucking the shit out of me to the point where I came only seconds after. Wrapping my dreads around his hand, he thrust into me with all his might, and had me crying out like a little ass baby.

"You like that rough shit, huh bitch?" he growled and went even harder.

"Ahhh, ahhh, Ha-Hakim, uuuuh!" I released again, even though I didn't want to.

"Fuck! You little nasty bitch. You got some good pussy!" he called out right before he roared like a grizzly bear and released. “Oh shit!” he panted as he slid out of me.

I sat there in the same position, not really knowing what the hell to think. I mean I wanted it rough, but not like that. He came back from the bathroom with a towel, and handed it over to me.

“That was good baby, damn.” He pecked me before slipping his boxers on and sitting down.

“Yep, perfect.”

Kimberlyn

I looked at myself in the bathroom mirror, and smiled at my costume. The Quintons' costume party was this weekend, and I could not wait. Although I was seven months along, I didn't look like it. Well not to me I didn't. I only went up one size higher than normal for this cheerleading uniform, and I looked great. Of course there was a small round bulge in my midsection, but it was cute, not huge. I combed my fresh press down, grabbed my pom-poms, then exited the bathroom.

I entered the bedroom to see TQ typing something on the computer. Since he didn't notice me right away, I cleared my throat to let him know my presence needed to be acknowledged. Looking up from his computer, that pretty smile covered his face as he closed his laptop and put it to the side.

"A sexy ass cheerleader," he commented.

"Thank you." I turned around to show him the back of it. I'd gotten it customized so that it read *Team TQ*.

"That's my favorite part. If you wear that with the watch and the necklace, niggas will have no choice but to recognize."

"That's what I want," I smiled.

"Have you ever slept with a cheerleader?" I neared him.

"Plenty, but they were never as pretty as you," he bit his lip.

I began removing the uniform, and once it was off, I put on my short nightshirt before climbing into the huge comfy bed next to him. He'd been a little glum these days, and I missed him being funny, rude, and talkative. I could tell he was trying to mask it, but because I knew him so well from spending so much time with him, I could see right through the mask.

"What's wrong?" I asked him as he stared straight ahead.

"Nothing," he squeezed my thigh.

"Yes, it is, you're never this quiet. I can tell that you're thinking hard about something and I wanna know what it is." I straddled his lap.

He half smiled but then it faded quickly as he caressed my belly.

"I was just thinking of something dumb," he chuckled lightly.

"What was it?"

He paused for a few moments before answering.

"I was thinking about how I had the chance to be raised by my maternal grandparents. I wonder if I would be a photographer instead of what I am now. A simple person; a regular person. A person who just wakes up, goes to work, and comes home."

"You don't like what you do?"

"I wouldn't say I like it or dislike it. It's just who I've always been. I've always been TQ, a Quinton, somebody important, and—it was just a thought I had, that's all. Let's talk about something else."

While still straddling him, I scooted my body closer into his and kissed his lips. I then hugged his neck tightly, and rubbed the back of his head to soothe him. He was loosely holding me at first, but he eventually hugged me tighter and kissed my neck. We hugged like that for what seemed like an eternity, and I had no plans on letting go.

***

I woke up to the smell of food, but it wasn't a familiar smell, so I didn't know what it was. Peeling the covers off, I got out of the bed and quickly made it up. I fluffed the pillows the way TQ liked, and then went into the bathroom to wash my face and brush my teeth. When I was done, I headed to the kitchen to see him cooking and bobbing his head to some rap music. He had on headphones but I could still hear. On his body were some basketball shorts, boxers, socks, and Jordan slides. His shirt was off and the sight of his strong back covered in tattoos had me a little hot and bothered.

I just sat at the bar, and watched him finish up whatever he was making. He finally turned around, and smiled widely when he saw me. It was nothing like seeing the man you love be happy to see you. He was so adorable, and I just loved everything about him.

"I made you food." He removed his headphones and let them hang from his neck.

"I didn't know you could cook."

"I'm only good with Russian food, eggs, bacon, steaks, ribs, and cereal."

"That's more than I can say for a lot of people. You're so well rounded. What is this?" I asked as I looked down at the dish.

"This is fried eggs with dill and kolbasa, which is like Russian sausage. And these are called syrniki, which are just like cottage cheese filled Russian pancakes, with honey and strawberries."

"Thanks, baby," I smiled as he handed me a fork and some juice, before sitting down with a plate for himself. I dug in immediately.

"How do you like it?"

"It's good, but why don't you ever eat scrambled eggs?" I questioned. Whenever I made breakfast for him, he always wanted fried eggs.

"I've never really eaten those growing up. My mother made them once but my dad made her toss them, because Russians don't typically eat those, according to him. My dad didn't let his children eat things he didn't like."

"Really? So if he didn't like cinnamon, you couldn't eat it?" I frowned and he nodded. "I've never heard that before."

"My dad is a strange man. I guess him being strange made his kids a bit strange too."

"Yes, but I love the way you are. I enjoy learning about your Russian culture."

"So you don't mind that we celebrate Christmas, January seventh?" he smirked.

"Not anymore. It was weird when you told me the first time, but now I think I can get with it. What will we do for the twenty-fifth of December?"

"We can open gifts and stuff, you and I, but the seventh is when we go to church and have a big Christmas party with the family. It'll be normal for you as the years go on. It's funny because seeing people celebrate on the twenty-fifth is weird for me."

"And hearing about it on the seventh is weird for me. But I guess since we're gonna be together, I don't mind it."

"We are. You're gonna be my wife and we're gonna be one big happy black and Russian family," he chuckled to himself as he sipped his juice.

"I can't wait." I leaned over to him, and he turned his face to kiss my lips.

"I love you, shorty," he said in between pecks.

"I love you too.

Britain

The night of the party…

"What do you think?" Goldie walked out in a tight white dress, with a halo on her head.

"You're an angel?" I frowned down at her. I felt like now that she was pregnant, she shouldn't be wearing tight shit like that.

"Yes, don't I look innocent?"

"No, not after what you were doing last night," I pulled her closer to me and kissed her soft lips. "I like when you wear your hair curly."

"I don't, too much maintenance. I just didn't have time to go and get my hair done, so this was the best that I could do."

"Well I like it. You should wear it like that more, for me."

"I guess since you're fine as fuck." She rolled her eyes and smacked her lips. "What are you?"

"Britain Quinton."

"Really? You told me you were gonna dress up! You're gonna be the only one who isn't wearing a costume!"

"No, the only people that dress up are a couple of my dad's workers, and the women. None of my brothers will be dressed up, I can promise you that."

"And you're sure you don't want me to ride with you?" she pouted.

"Nah, shorty. Ride with your friends and I will come in a little later. You can leave with me though," I pecked her again and then patted my pockets to make sure I had everything I needed.

We both left the house once Summer pulled up to get her, and I really didn't understand why she was coming but whatever. She and my brother weren't even cool, but I guess since she was invited every year, she didn't want to miss it. Our parties were always the talk of the town the day after, and because the guest list was exclusive, people always wanted to find a way to get in. That's if they even heard about it in time. You had to know the right people to even find out that we were having a function. So in a way, I guess I understood why Summer still wanted to attend. There would be plenty of muthafuckas there though, so she and Rhys wouldn't have to speak. Also, Rhys would be very occupied with Indiya, I'm sure.

I locked up my condo, and then went down to get into my car. I was gonna pick up the weed for the party, and just in case some shit popped off and I got caught, I didn't want my shorty in the car with me. Unlike my father, I didn't want my lady dabbling in this shit, because what good would we be to our children if we both get locked up? Plus, I wanted my shorty to enjoy the fruits of my labor, not work for it too. And I liked that she had her own goals separate from mine.

As soon as I pulled out of the parking structure of my condo, three police cars came out of nowhere. One blocked me from the front, and there were two more behind me to make sure I didn't reverse the other way I guess. Throwing my car into park, all kinds of shit ran through my mind as I wondered what the hell all of this was for. I mean three police officers? What the hell could this possibly be about? I knew it had nothing to do with the crime family because we had that shit completely under control.

One of the officers walked towards my vehicle and wound his hand to tell me to roll the window down. I did as he asked, but kept looking straight because I didn't want to acknowledge him. *Please let one of these niggas be on my father's payroll.*

"Britain Quinton?" he asked as he looked at a paper.

"Is there a problem?"

"Step out of the car, Mr. Quinton."

"Oh my gosh, yo." I shut the engine off and got out of the car. As soon as I did, one of the other officers slammed me into my vehicle, and began patting me down. "What is this for!" I hollered.

"Britain Quinton, you're under arrest for the murder of Tekeya Mitchell's unborn child, also known as feticide. You have the right..."

Are you fucking serious right now? Why didn't I murk that bitch?

CHAPTER TWELVE

At the party…

I held onto Kimberlyn's waist as we walked into the mansion party together. There were so many people here already, and I just wanted to get her up to the VIP area so she would be safe while I went and talked to my brothers. As we were passing people, speaking here and there, I saw Jayce walking up, grinning. This muthafucka was on my shit list, and I had no interest in speaking to him at the moment. I hated for Rhys to be right about him being fake, but I was starting to feel the same way as him.

"TQ, man, what's up? Kimberlyn, you look beautiful," he smiled. My shorty knew not to speak to him, so we both just stared. "Aye man, I know I've been MIA, but I was going through something. I'm good now though, and I wanted to talk to you."

"Shorty, go over to the VIP area with your friends and stay close with them for the whole party, okay?"

"Where are you going?" she asked.

"I'll be around, but until I come get you, stay with them, okay?" I looked down at her and she nodded. I pecked her lips, and watched her walk off before looking back to Jayce. "Fuck do you want to talk about? Why are you even here?"

"I wanted to talk about how you plan on getting back at Gang for what he did to Kimberlyn."

"How do you know what he did?" I frowned.

"Because he told me what he did."

"What are you talking to him for?"

"He tried to get me to be on his team to go against you but I declined. But before that, he explained that he needed my help because the guy he'd hired failed."

"Well, I already have something in motion so I don't need your help." I started to walk off and he followed me.

"You could always use an extra man. When do you plan on attacking him?"

I stopped in my tracks, and then turned to face him.

"Jayce, get the fuck out of my face before I break yours, aight?" I raised a brow and he just nodded in agreement, before heading towards the door. Yes, please leave.

As I walked by Lendsey and Rhys, I waved them to follow me to the poolroom. Once inside, I locked the door and took a deep breath. Tonight my life would change, and after much hard thinking, I knew it was worth it. I had three jobs in my relationship, and that was to provide for Kimberlyn, secure her, and make sure she was happy. If I failed to do any one of the three, my success with the others would be in vain. Letting Gang live to avoid confrontation with my father would be me failing at securing her, and I refused to do that.

"So what's the deal?" Lendsey asked.

"Where is Britain?" I frowned and checked my watch.

"Nigga said he was just going to pick up some weed but he still ain't here. I'm sure he will be here soon," Lendsey replied.

"Aight, well the plan worked. Gang is expecting to meet with Burke tonight. What he doesn't know, is that I'm showing up to the meeting as well."

Burke was this guy that I'd hired to basically get in good with Gang. I coached him on all the right things to say, because I knew Gang was looking for a replacement for Peel. He couldn't run that shit alone, and Burke was the perfect candidate. Tonight they were meeting at Gang's warehouse to discuss business, mainly what they were gonna do after they killed me in case they lost my dad as a connect. You would think that my dad would cut him off if I was killed, but I honestly couldn't say if he would display such loyalty.

"I'm coming with you, just in case," Rhys said.

"Rhys, I don't need any backup. Gang is nothing."

"What if he has men there?"

"He won't because he doesn't take men with him to meetings. He will bring one gunman or security guy with him, but nothing else. I can kill two niggas in a split second, so whomever he brings won't be a problem either."

"Will Burke be prepared to shoot if it comes down to it?" Lendsey asked. "He needs to be. Tarenz, just let one of us come."

"No, I got it. And this is not something I want to drag y'all into. You know once I body Gang, Pops is gonna be furious, so I don't want you guys on the other end of his wrath. Let me do this alone. This is about *my* girl, and therefore it's *my* problem."

"Well either way, we're gonna be going down together because we ain't gon' let Dad come at you, TQ," Rhys replied.

"Hell nah. We're brothers, fuck that nigga," Lendsey added.

I was happy to know they'd have my back, but still, this was my battle. If I could save my brothers from becoming an enemy of my father's, then I would. My dad didn't change his first name to Stony just because it sounded nice. He changed it because it described his character in every way. He could kill all his sons and sleep like a newborn that same night. That's just the type of dude he was, and I guess that's why he'd been so successful.

"Glad to know who y'all would ride for. But aye, I have to go. Stay by the girls, and call Britain if he don't show up soon, okay?"

"You know he's gon' be mad we didn't force ourselves onto the trip, right?" Lendsey raised a brow.

"He'll be aight," I said as we chuckled. We dapped and hugged one another, before we all exited the poolroom.

I passed the section where my shorty and her friends were, and she gave me that big beautiful smile of hers before blowing me a kiss.

That gave me more ammo to do what I had to do tonight; this was for her.

***

Pulling up to the warehouse in my '95 Ford Explorer with New York Plates, I quickly shut the engine off and twisted on my silencer. I'd changed out of my tuxedo fit, and into a jogger suit in black. I had on some Nike Roshe sneakers just in case, gloves, and a skullcap. My dummy phone buzzed, and I looked down to see it was a message from Burke.

B: *Everything is a go. Come in at any moment using the door to the right of the warehouse… it's open. As soon as you walk in, you will see us sitting at a round table a little ways away. He has one guy here, but he's scrawny. Lol.*

What kind of nigga puts LOL to another nigga? I don't know, but that's a discussion for another day I guess. I wouldn't correct it now because there were more important things at hand, but if he started sending emojis we would have a problem.

I crept up on the side, and spotted the door that Burke told me to look for. Slipping my dummy phone into a pouch attached to my bulletproof vest, I slowly turned the knob of the door. It was open just like Burke said it would be, and I stepped in gently before closing it behind me. I glanced around briefly, and didn't see anyone on the sides of me. When I looked straight ahead, I spotted Burke and Gang sitting at a round table talking. I began walking towards them briskly, while still making sure not to make much noise.

PHEW! PHEW!

I sent two bullets into the side of Gang's head, and smiled because he never saw it coming.

"About time you showed up," Burke smiled and stood to his feet.

POP!

I saw a bullet fly into Burke's forehead, causing him to drop dead immediately. I turned around quickly to see who had killed him, but a pistol greeted me, digging into my forehead. *Fuck!* I shouted in my head as he cocked the gun, preparing to splatter my brains.

My last words were, "For real, Jayce?"

TO BE CONTINUED

CPSIA information can be obtained
at www.ICGtesting.com
Printed in the USA
LVOW10s1331300817
546968LV00022BA/579/P